I0571194

INTO THE DARK

TALES FROM THE LIGHTHOUSE
BOOK 2

D.L. STRAND

Storyteller's
PUBLISHING

For my girls, Alyssa and Kayla -
Here's another reason for you to ask your mom,
"What's wrong with dad?"

For my wife, Monika -
Without you, my life would truly be a horror story.

1

A THREAT

Lightning flashed the world into existence, then sent it back into a darkness filled with jagged afterimages, as thunder rocked the ground beneath my feet.

I stood atop a massive rock in the middle of the boiling sea, holding my best friend upright, my hands clasped tight around her waist, as we faced the wild night. Below, waves pounded the cliff upon which we stood, shuddering the stone and blasting a torrent of water up the wall, to rain back down upon us, heavy and ice cold, threatening to wash us into the frigid depths. Looming over us from behind, silent and implacable, stood the lighthouse.

Max was unconscious, or worse, while I was helpless - a passenger in my own body. Unable to do anything but watch as my own limbs sought to end her life.

In my head I screamed, "No," but my mouth wouldn't utter a word. I struggled to regain control but there was no lever to pull. No button to press. It was as if I was adrift in water or space, without anything to get ahold of. Nothing to push, punch, or kick. Still, I fought on. I begged my limbs to obey - to stop, or for God's sake to simply step back.

Instead, all I could do was watch as my hands, free of my control, traveled around to her back, and, to my horror, pushed.

Like a rag doll, she pitched forward and fell, bouncing off the pitted wall twice, before disappearing into the water below.

I trembled, and the world trembled with me.

"Wake the fuck up."

Freezing wind and rain morphed into stiff fabric sheets against my skin. Ocean brine and ozone were replaced by the stench of day-old coffee breath and stale cigars.

"Come on."

The stormy scene evaporated and a blurry form filled my vision.

"You little shit!"

The words bounced off my brain like an angry brick off a rubber wall. "Huh? What?" I'm not the most eloquent when I first wake up. Still half in my dream, I struggled with reality.

"She's your best friend." Spit sprinkled my face as the rough voice punctuated each word.

The gel in front of my eyes solidified into a familiar face. "Mr. Morales? Where am I?" The walls were mint green and the air smelled of antiseptic. A curtain curved around my bed. "Is this a hospital? What're you doing here?" Suddenly I was awake. "Max? Is she—?"

"No, she's not okay, you little snot-fucker. You beat the shit out of her."

Max was alive. It had been a dream. I hadn't killed her after all.

With that realization, circuits closed, and I found myself fully in the here and now.

The last thing I remembered was getting rescued from the damned lighthouse by a fisherman trolling by. Max and I had been through hell. We were lucky to have survived.

"Where is she?"

"None of your Goddamned business, and if I have my way—"

"Mr. Morales, you said you were going to ask the boy some questions." A nurse stood behind him. I hadn't noticed her.

"Damned right I am. What the fuck set you off—?"

"Mr. Morales, Sam's been through a lot. Can you take it down a bit?"

"Sure, I'll take it down," he yelled, "just as soon as I throw his ass in jail for what he did to my daughter."

Max's dad was an intimidating guy on the best days. He wasn't tall, but he was solid. Not the kind of solid you see in the gym, rather the kind of solid that puts criminals onto the ground - face first - hard.

"Mr. Morales, Sam has a concussion, lacerations on his face and arms. Contusions all over his body, and a serious penetration wound to his leg."

"Of course he does. My little girl isn't a fucking pussy. He's lucky she didn't kill him. C'mon, you little shit, tell me why."

He wasn't wrong. Max had done her best to kill me. Well, not Max exactly. I mean, yes, she'd held the knife, but she hadn't been in control of herself. For that matter, neither had I. It's a long story.

There was no way I could tell him I wasn't responsible for Max's condition. I mean, I was. But then again, I wasn't. Honestly, I hadn't sorted it out in my own head yet.

"Detective, I'm going to have to ask you to leave," said the nurse.

"Like hell you are."

"Now, Mr. Morales." There was steel in her voice. She strode to the door and opened it. He was a difficult person to stand up to.

He gave her a sideways glance. "Fine." He leaned down into my face. "The minute you're out on the street, your ass is mine." He straightened his coat, then stormed out.

She let the door swing shut behind him, then came over and plumped my pillow. Her manner was gentle, efficient.

I lifted my head. The pain came on fast, forcing me to squeeze my eyes shut and lay back.

"Take it slow," she said gently.

"Where's Max?" I asked through the discomfort. The last time I'd seen her, we were helping each other limp up the dock, ecstatic to be back on the mainland, free of the lighthouse. Alive. After that, the world went dark, and the next thing I knew, her dad was making like Sergeant Carter to my slack-faced Gomer Pyle.

"She's resting." She held up a finger to stop me from interrupting. "She's going to be fine. So will you, if you give yourself a chance."

"Can I see her?"

"Not right now." The last word carried a hint of the hardness she'd used on Mr. Morales. "In the meantime, I'll call your grandmother. She'll want to know you're awake. She's hardly left your side since you arrived."

"Gram?" Guilt swept through me like a wave. What was I going to tell her?

"How long have I been out?"

"Two days."

That was a relief. I was afraid she'd say months, or years. I have an active imagination.

"Yes, and you'll be here for a few more if you don't take it easy." She reached over to my I.V. and made an adjustment.

I started to ask another question, but couldn't remember what it was. The room lost focus, and I sank into my dreams.

2

AN OUTING

The following night's sleep was no more restful. Images of storms and blood and rusty blades filled my dreams. I awoke exhausted, out of breath - as though I'd spent the entire night fleeing something. It wasn't hard to imagine what.

I awoke with the sheets clinging to my sweaty body, restricting my limbs. It brought back memories of Max sitting on top of me, her knees pinning my arms to my sides, holding the bloody knife above her head, poised to strike again.

I opened my eyes. Sunlight streamed through the window, casting a harsh light across the room. I blinked, trying to bring things into focus.

A woman with steel-gray hair, wearing a purple jogging suit, sat in the chair next to the bed. She looked worn, as though she hadn't slept. It creaked as she leaned forward and patted my leg.

"Gram." I hadn't seen my grandmother since my ... uh ... *adventure*. Relief and guilt fought for dominance in my head.

"I'm sorry," I said.

She placed her hand over mine and squeezed. Her skin was tough, covered in calluses from years spent tending our home and garden. Her small gesture implied that I was okay, and that was all that mattered. She held a cup for me, and I sipped from the straw. The water soothed my throat.

I took a deep breath, trying to calm my mind. It still didn't seem real, being back - safe. Well, safe as long as Max's dad kept his distance.

"How's Max?" I asked.

She rolled her eyes. It seemed Max was full of the devil, as usual.

Gram didn't talk. She hadn't spoken since we lost my grandpa a couple of years before. Still, she made herself understood.

"Can I see her?" I asked.

She shrugged her shoulders, patted my hand, and mimed falling asleep.

But I'd slept enough. There was so much Max and I needed to talk about. We'd almost killed each other, after all.

What was I supposed to tell her? That the ghost of some psychotic serial killer haunted the old lighthouse, keeping watch over the remains of his family? That he and the daughter he'd murdered had used our bodies to wage some kind of war against each other?

I shifted in my bed. Pain shot through my leg. I couldn't tell anyone what had happened. Not until we'd had the chance to talk.

The door swung inward; a different nurse entered soundlessly.

Her black hair was cut short, and she wore large, red-rimmed glasses that covered half her face. She had an air of efficiency, as most nurses do, but there was something lighter about her demeanor - a slight smirk, as if she knew the punchline to a joke she hadn't shared with the rest of the class. Tiny rhinestones rimmed her name tag: Constance Higgins, RN.

Gram smiled and shook her head.

"Ah, we're awake. How're we doing, Mr. Freman?"

"I want to see my friend," I said.

Nurse Higgins looked to Gram for clarification.

"Max - Maxine Morales," I said. She's a patient here,"

"Ah. I'm sure you'll be able to visit her soon. Right now, we need to see how you're doing."

She grabbed the chart from its place on the door and flipped through the pages.

"You've had quite the time."

The whole thing was my fault. It'd been Max's idea to go out on the water, but it was my boat. I'd had the final say. If I'd checked the forecast, I would've known bad weather was on the way. Hell, there were signs, but I couldn't tell Max no. I had trouble telling anyone no. I was such a fucking pushover.

Anyway, we'd taken my boat out despite my better judgment. Then, as Max would've said, shit went sideways.

"When do you think I'll be able to get up and walk around?" I asked.

"Let's start small. Feel up to a little tour of the hospital?" She stepped outside the room and returned with a wheelchair.

I sat up - too quickly, apparently. It felt like my brain was trying to break out of my skull with a claw hammer. I collapsed back onto my pillow.

"Easy, tiger. Let's try that again. Slow it down this time."

She gave me a moment to catch my breath, reached behind my head, and gently helped me sit up. Once she was sure I'd stay vertical, she turned back the covers and guided my legs over the side. We paused while I adjusted to this new position. My head swam, but it wasn't overwhelming.

She guided my hands around her neck, wrapped me in her arms, and moved me gently down into the wheelchair. The vinyl chilled my exposed back. Thankfully, she'd provided a cushion to sit on. My butt still stung from where I'd burned it. Don't ask - it's a long story.

"You okay?"

I'd worked up a sweat, but yeah, I was okay. I nodded.

She unfolded the foot rests and guided my feet onto them.

"Would you like to come along?" she asked Gram, who shook her head and waved us off.

"Looks like it's you and me." She rolled me out into the hall. It was alive with organized activity: doctors and nurses checking charts, discussing patients, rushing from one place to another. After spending so much time alone in the room, and before that, the lighthouse, where it was just Max and me, (and a couple of pissed-off ghosts) I found the activity reassuring. Being around other people put me at ease as she wheeled me around the floor.

"Anywhere you'd like to go?"

"McDonald's?" It wasn't easy to joke.

"Maybe next trip."

"I'd like to see Max."

"Right. Your friend. Let's see." She wheeled me to the nurse's station. From down where I sat, it looked like a large block, made from strips of light wood. Stuck in the wheelchair, I wasn't tall enough to see anyone behind it.

"Clara, could you check on a patient? Uh, Maxine Morales." She looked at me for confirmation. I nodded.

"Sure," Clara said, a smile in her voice. I liked Clara - so helpful. I heard the controlled clatter of her fingers on a keyboard.

"Looks like they released her earlier this morning."

Strike one for Clara.

Nurse Higgins looked down at me and pursed her lips. "Sorry, tiger. It looks like she's going to have to come find you. Anywhere else you'd like to go?"

Defeated, I shrugged my shoulders.

"The cafeteria it is." She wheeled me into the elevator and pressed the "B" button. We were the only ones in the car as we sank down to the basement. Hidden speakers played an electronic version of the song 'Beth' by Kiss.

Our descent slowed, then a bell chimed as the doors opened, and out I rolled. It was a big room, well-lit by windows running down the length of it. The space churned with hospital staff, patients and visitors. The scent of burgers and french fries met me as I rolled in, but they didn't smell appetizing at all. In fact, they had the opposite effect.

"What's your pleasure?"

My stomach clenched. "I-I'm not hungry."

"You sure? I'm buying. That doesn't happen often. Ask anyone."

"I'm sure." I hadn't followed most of what she'd said. "Can you take me back?" The room warmed suddenly. Sweat trickled down my neck. I felt off-balance.

She came around, knelt down and stared at me through narrowed eyes. "You feeling okay?"

"I'm fine!" I snapped. I took a breath, trying to get on top of whatever this was. "Please, take me back to my room." What was happening?

"Sure." She pivoted the chair and retraced our brief trip, back to the elevator. The call button lit up when she touched it.

My heart hammered fast and heavy in my chest.

"You sure you're okay?"

I nodded, but kept my eyes on the elevator doors. What was the holdup? I closed my eyes and clutching the arms of the wheelchair, tried to calm myself.

The light murmur of voices and the clatter of silverware mixed with the roar of blood rushing through my head.

She whispered next to my ear. "Take a slow, deep breath." Her voice added to the chaos of sensations colliding in my mind.

I had to get out. I opened my eyes, searching the room for an escape route. My breath came in quick gasps.

"Sam, slow down. Breathe."

Why did she keep saying that? I was breathing. Too much, in fact. I couldn't get enough air into my lungs.

I sought desperately for a way out. A few feet away from the elevator was a door with an exit sign and a jagged graphic that symbolized either a stairway — or a stick figure walking up a lightning bolt. I placed my feet on the floor and rose halfway out of my chair. The room turned sideways. A mac truck slammed into the back of my head, and I fell over, taking the wheelchair with me.

"Sam!" Her voice reached me from a distance.

I landed hard on the cold floor, panting like a fish wrenched from the water. I raised my head, and my gut emptied itself onto the linoleum. As my body rejected my breakfast, my skull threatened to crack wide open.

The room darkened. Everything faded to black.

3

MAX

I awoke sometime later with an aching head. My mouth tasted like puke, but the bed stayed beneath me, so that was a plus.

"What kind of pansy-ass shit is this?" Dark hair shaved on one side, the other side tipped in red. The piercings in her face sparkled in the fluorescent light.

"Max!" My voice sounded rough, weak, as if my lungs lacked the strength to push the gunk out of my throat.

"Your breath smells like ass." She made a face and reached over to the tray next to my bed. grabbed the small plastic cup and held it for me.

The water helped. I closed my eyes and breathed relief. When I opened them, I could see more clearly. She'd covered her bruises with heavy makeup. Her nose looked engorged, and she wore extra concealer under her eyes.

She still looked great.

"Your dad—"

"—is convinced you tried to kill me. As if!"

"Max, I'm s—"

"Fuck you."

"So, we're okay?"

She offered the cup for me to take another sip. "Let's move on before our periods sync up."

"No, I'm serious. After the fight and everything - I want to make sure."

"Okay, you were a bit of an asshole, but I'm used to that."

"As long as—"

"We're fine. Now, is there a Tic Tac or something around here, 'cause damn!"

I chuckled, which hurt, but I was relieved we were good. "Not much I can do. How're you feeling? Are things okay at home?"

She set the cup down. "I'm fine. You're fine. We can move on, okay?"

"Okay, I was just, you know, worried about how things went with your stepmom."

"We're fine," she repeated, a little too loudly.

"Really? She forgave you?"

"For her cat? As far as she knows, the little shit ran away, or was attacked by a dog or something."

"So, you're not telling her."

She rolled her eyes and exhaled. "What's up with your boat?"

It took a moment for me to adjust to the change of subject. "It's still in the marina, I guess - in pretty bad shape."

"Maybe we can go see it. When are you getting out of here?"

"I think they want to make sure I don't pass out or puke or anything when the wind changes."

She nodded. "By the way, Charlie's been asking 'bout you."

Charlie ran The Wave, a local diner where we hung out.

"Cool. Tell him I said hi."

"He's got a cute new waitress. You'd like her."

"Why would I like her?"

"I told you, she's cute."

I laughed, then winced, which made her laugh. It felt good to see my best friend again.

4

HOME!

My head felt like it was filled with helium as Max pulled onto Ocean View Terrace, then stopped in front of our house. She slammed her door and strode around the front of her truck, an old, 1960's heap she'd rehabbed using discarded parts she'd scrounged from the local junkyard and auto shops around town. It was mostly red and sounded like a beast.

She opened my door, grabbed my crutches from the back, and held them out for me while I slowly slid off the vinyl seat and touched down on the curb. This was going to be my first real test using them - a necessary evil if I wanted my leg to heal. They almost hadn't let me leave the hospital, given the extent of my injuries, my bouts of anxiety, and lack of coordination. I had to assure them the last issue had always been iffy.

Regarding the anxiety, back when I was in high school, I'd had to stay alert, going from one class to another, keeping my eyes peeled for Mitch Kavenaugh, my personal tormentor. I always expected him or one of his cronies to ambush me with a lifter or stuff me into a locker, or worse. That was anxiety. What I experienced in the hospital - that was real fear. Terror. They call them panic attacks for a reason.

Max held open the gate of our picket fence while I worked my wobbly way up the walk. I wasn't dizzy, exactly, just not quite balanced.

Our small yard made for one hell of a welcome home. The garden was Gram's refuge - a patchwork of different shades of vivid green. Our massive hydrangea bush obscuring the small porch was the star of the show with its football-sized leaves and massive pink and powder-blue blossoms.

The door opened, and Gram stepped out, smiling.

She and Max made a big production of my entrance. She held the screen door open as Max followed me up the short flight of stairs, guiding me with her hand on my back. There were just four steps. Still, I almost lost my balance twice. It didn't help that the earth insisted on tipping sideways.

I squeezed through the door and stood in the entryway, between the living room on my right and the dining room on my left.

"Fuckin' A." Max wiped her brow in mock relief.

Ahead of me was the hallway leading to the bedrooms, and Gram ushered me toward the back of the house, expecting me to follow.

I had other ideas. I turned right and headed toward our comfy old couch. In my mind, I pictured myself just flopping down like I always did. But once I got there, I realized this was going to be harder than I thought. I now had three legs, essentially. Two of them didn't bend, and the other one wasn't particularly strong. I stood, staring down at my refuge, puzzling out in my medicated brain how this was going to work.

Gram hadn't moved. She stamped her feet. Her face was stern, her arms folded. She freed a hand and pointed toward my bedroom.

Here's the thing. While I was away, first at the lighthouse and then at the hospital, the one thing I looked forward to was coming home. That probably isn't surprising. But, as much as I liked my room, for me, home meant sitting on the couch in front of the TV. That was the image that kept me going. Oh, and Gram, of course. I cried actual tears at the prospect of never seeing her again. But I did not fantasize about being closed off in my bedroom. In the hospital,

I'd spent quite enough time alone with my thoughts, thank you. Now, I just wanted to turn off my brain and watch some Phil Donahue. I didn't want to think about what had happened.

"Dude." Max looked uncomfortable with this standoff.

"I want to sit on the couch."

Gram snatched up a stack of papers from the table and shook it at me. Included in there somewhere was a list of requirements from the doctor, including my prescriptions, and, I'm sure, a scribble that specified bed rest.

"What's the difference as long as I'm taking it easy?" I turned my butt towards the couch, put my crutches in front of me, and lowered myself down. I got about halfway when my leg gave out. The sudden jolt as I hit the cushions sent pain shooting to every corner of my skull. I winced. "Ow!"

Resigned, Gram smacked the papers back down on the dining room table and stalked off to the back of the house.

Max clapped her hands together once. "Well you seem to be okay. I should go check in at work."

"Later," I said. "Oh, and thanks."

"Hasta." She closed the door behind her.

Gram came back with a blanket, a pillow, and a look of resignation. She helped arrange me on the couch and then pointed at the TV and wagged her finger.

"But..."

She put her hands on her hips and shook her head. I saw there was no negotiating this point. She tilted her head to the side and closed her eyes in a pantomime of sleeping.

"I'm not tired."

With her lips drawn tight, she cocked her head and nodded toward my room. She was pretty clear. I could sleep here or there. Those were my choices.

At least I was on the couch. I knew Gram would walk back and forth as she straightened the house, doing whatever she needed to. It felt comforting to know that there was going to be a little activity around me.

I exhaled. "Fine."

She shot me a critical look.

"Really!" I put my head down on the pillow and closed my eyes, convinced I was not going to sleep.

Sometime later, I awoke to Gram shaking my shoulder. She held a couple of pills and a glass of water.

Still groggy, I popped the pills into my mouth and washed them down, then laid my head back. The next thing I knew, it was morning, and she was waking me up for breakfast.

The following days were replays of the first. I floated in and out of consciousness as my body spent most of its energy healing.

It took me back to when I was in grade school, before my parents died. Spending my sick days on the couch. Back then, it was comforting, reclining under a blanket, with a bowl of soup next to me, or grilled cheese, or a TV dinner, watching talk shows in the morning and 'Dialing for Dollars' in the afternoon. To be clear, I wasn't always sick. Sometimes I just needed to spend some time away from school and be looked after. I'm not sure what that says about me. I don't care.

The important thing was, I was home.

5

MY BOAT

OVER THE NEXT FEW DAYS, MY BODY HEALED AND I GOT STRONGER. Eventually, Gram insisted I move off the couch and back to my bed.

When I was awake, and I felt my mind drifting back to that night, I'd open a comic book, or make a fist and pound my bed or whatever. I'd do anything to avoid thinking about it, spending my time reading or engrossed in TV, while she puttered around the house or worked in the garden.

Max's dad stopped by a few times to find out exactly what had happened - he said. I didn't know what to tell him. While he intimidated the hell out of me, he didn't scare Gram. She didn't let him past the front door.

Max and I needed to get our story straight. The truth was too insane. Two spirits carjacking our bodies to wage a supernatural proxy war with each other is not something you go spreading around town.

The skipper who'd rescued us from the island had been kind enough to make arrangements to salvage Grandpa's boat, so Max offered to drive me to the marina to take a look. My stomach was buzzing like a wasp hive. I knew it was going to be bad.

"Explain to me again why you don't have a fucking driver's license." Max seemed happy to be out and about. I think things'd gotten pretty tense around her house.

"I guess I haven't had the time."

"You graduated last year. You don't work. Besides playing video games and fishing, you don't have any hobbies. What takes up your time?"

"Fishing and playing video games," I said. "By the way, how did your stepmom take the news about her cat?"

She shot me a look. "Fuck you."

I felt a little guilty bringing it up. Max and Eartha Kitty - yes, that was the cat's name - hadn't gotten along. The short version was, Max had taken their little feud too far. The cat freaked, and ran out into the street. That's the reason we'd been out on the water that night. She'd wanted to dump its body in the bay - a burial at sea.

We pulled in to the marina parking lot - a flat space next to the docks, covered with gravel. The tires crunched over the loose surface as we found our space and stopped.

The sun had yet to peek out, staying hidden behind a full cover of clouds, so the air carried the chill of morning. An ancient sign hung rusting on the chain-link fence: faded red letters read, *Santa Carla Marina* on a splotchy white background. We walked past it and into the yard. Once inside, we were surrounded by boats of varying ages, in different states of disrepair. Some hadn't touched the water in decades - permanent monuments to the costs of ownership.

An elderly man exited the corrugated steel quonset hut and waddled over to meet us. His grizzled white beard and ruddy complexion told of a life spent outdoors. He sheathed his hands in the top of his ancient, faded denim overalls. From his lips hung a half-smoked cigarette. He smiled around it as he came to greet us.

"Sam?"

"Hi Dale, this is my friend, Max."

He regarded her for a moment, then stuck out his hand.

She shook it.

Still smiling, he grasped my hand tight in his rough, calloused grip.

"I remember when it was all I could do to keep you from climbing on the old wrecks"

Grampa used to come here to shop for odds and ends. Dale was always trying to sell him a bigger boat.

"I can't believe you're still trolling around in your granddad's ol' skiff," he said.

"Old habits."

He chuckled at that. "That's what he used to say." He gestured with his cigarette. "She's over here." He led the way around the back of the rounded steel building. "He was a good friend. About broke my heart when he passed. How's your gramma?"

"She's good. She says hi." Actually, she didn't know I was coming, but it seemed the polite thing to say.

Gulls laughed from above as we came to a stop, and I saw my boat, tossed against the fence, leaning between a pair of weathered cabin cruisers. It lay on its side, facing us. The engine and gas tanks were missing.

"Your granddad and I shared a lot of beers in this boat. It's a shame."

My heart froze. "Shame?"

He pulled on the top edge and let it fall. It landed face-down with a metallic crash. The aluminum hull still carried the scars and stains from years on the sea. *Dorothy* (Gram's name) was spelled out in faded black letters.

Dale pointed at the keel, now bashed in, the metal ripped open.

He pulled the cigarette from between his teeth and wedged it between his short thick fingers. "Your granddad sure enjoyed her. I'm sorry, son."

"You can't fix it?"

"Sure I can," he said, "but it's just not worth it. You can buy two boats for what it's going to cost. Best to let her go. She's served long and faithful."

It was worse than I thought. I didn't have the money to pay for repairs anyway, let alone a new boat.

Through my own poor judgement, I had lost a very personal

link to the man who raised me. It was hard to breathe. I couldn't bear to let it go. "Can I think about it?"

"Sure. I'll need your answer by the end of the week though, otherwise I'm going to have to charge for storage."

Max was uncharacteristically quiet.

"I've got the motor back in the shop," he continued. " It'll take some doing, but I can fix it. I could take her off your hands for say, fifty bucks."

"Don't do him any fuckin' favors." Max spit the words at him as she grabbed my arm and pulled me toward the gate. "C'mon."

Dale's eyes widened like he'd been shot.

"Max!" I was mortified.

"Don't touch a thing, you goddamned ghoul," she shouted back at him. "We'll figure it out ourselves." She stomped back to her truck and had it started before I'd opened the passenger door. I tossed my crutches in the back and climbed in.

I didn't know what to say. I stared at Dale's surprised face as she jammed the truck into reverse, backed out of the space, and then slammed the stick into first. We sped out of the parking lot in a hail of gravel, fishtailed onto the road, and headed downtown.

"What was that about? He's a friend."

"Bullshit! He's an asshole."

"What're we gonna do now?"

"You're not giving him your boat."

"Giving? Didn't you hear him? It's done. He offered—"

"—I heard what he offered. That motor's worth ten times that. It just needs some work, maybe a new prop. I don't know. At any rate, you're not giving it to that fucking butt-munch."

I strapped the seatbelt across my lap as we sped down the road. There was no point in talking right now. Her gears were turning faster than the car's.

6

THE WAVE

At first, I thought Max was taking me home. Instead, she drove downtown and pulled up in front of our diner.

The Wave was busy for a late Monday morning. Businessmen, surfers, and kids our age filled the place. It was a genuine neighborhood hangout. We fell into our regular booth. Weathered burgundy vinyl screeched as we both scooted into our usual seats.

Charlie waved a spatula at us from his place in front of the stove. He always looked like he'd just gotten out of bed, jumped on his Harley and rolled to work. He was big - taller than six feet and easily weighed over three hundred pounds. As always, he wore a white t-shirt covered by his stained apron, and an Oakland A's baseball cap.

In all the time we'd been coming here, we'd yet to figure out his job. Sure, he was the cook, but did he manage the place? Did he own it? We waved back.

Soon, a waitress came over with a couple of menus. I hadn't seen her before. Her name tag read *Jessica*.

"Can I get you something to drink?" Her voice was light - a little tentative.

Max didn't bother looking at the menu. "Hi, Jessica, I'll have a plate of fries and a Coke, no ice. Give him pancakes and eggs - scrambled - a Sprite, and your phone number." She flashed an evil smile at me.

I laughed nervously. "Max!" My face warmed. I wanted to squirm away. Jessica seemed embarrassed too. She smiled self-consciously. Her cheeks reddened. It was a good look for her.

"I'm sorry," I said. "She's off her meds."

She let loose with a small giggle. "I'll come back with your drinks."

Max leaned her head sideways, openly checking her out as she walked away. "Nice ass."

"Knock it off!" I hissed. The couple at the booth across from us looked up as if I'd yelled at them.

"See? She's your type,"

"What do you mean?"

"She talked to you. Your type."

I laughed. She knew me well.

"Shit." Max's face fell.

I turned to see a muscular blond douchebag push open the glass door and step inside. He was tall - really tall - and he wore his acid-washed jeans and Izod shirt like they'd been made for him. He shot a cruel smile at me as the door closed behind him and headed to our table.

I turned back toward Max. "Kill me now."

"Hey, ladies. I mean, lady, and Max." He pointed at my crutches. "You break your leg, Fremen?"

Max smiled. "Hey, Kavenaugh. How's your head?"

The two of them had tangled on the docks the day of our adventure. He'd gotten the worst of it.

His smile evaporated. "I owe you for that."

She looked around him. "Really? I don't see your backup."

"Excuse me." Jessica squeezed past him and set our drinks down in front of us, along with silverware and napkins. She'd set the straws in our sodas with the paper wrapper still covering the ends. It was a nice touch.

Kavenaugh regarded her the way a lion eyes a spring faun.

She turned toward him. "Will you be joining your friends? I could get another—"

He reached to her chest and grabbed her name tag, making a show of tilting it up so he could read it.

She froze.

"Jessica, eh? You're new here." He smiled his greasy smile.

"Kavenaugh, shouldn't you be in the pound with the other neutered bitches?" Max's voice was low and even but the look on her face implied imminent violence.

For the second time, his slimy smile disappeared. He glared at her as he let the name tag slip from between his fingers.

"I'll be back with your order," Jessica said as she escaped.

Max stood up. "Get lost."

"Dude, I—"

"—Your stink's wrecking my appetite. Fuck. Off." Her voice rose.

The other diners stopped what they were doing. The air tightened. She stepped so close to him her chest touched his stomach. Her neck craned upward, yet she managed to stare him down.

him down.

Kavenaugh stepped back, raising his hands. "Hey, easy. I was just saying hi."

She didn't blink.

"Fine. I'll go." Then he looked over at me. "Watch your back, Freman."

What the hell had I done?

He spun around and headed toward the door.

Max waited for him to clear the threshold then exhaled and relaxed back into her seat.

"Neutered bitches?" I laughed, still a little unnerved by the encounter. "Nice!"

We high-fived. For her, the incident seemed already forgotten.

A few minutes later, Jessica brought our food. It was simple, but smelled amazing.

Max picked up the ketchup, shook it hard, then twisted off the cap and dumped a huge glop on her fries. "Jessica, you new in town?"

"We just moved here," she replied. "It's closer to my dad's work. How about you?" She seemed a little flummoxed, but who could blame her after Idiot Boy's little exhibition?

"Do we look like tourists?" Max said as she bit a fry in half.

Jessica glanced at me. Max took a sip of her Coke, eyeballing me over the rim of her glass.

This was a perfect time for me to say something like, "What does your dad do?" or "Where did you move from?" or, "How do you like it here?" but my mind was blank.

Max jumped in. "I'm Max. I work at an auto shop a couple of blocks away. Sam here, goes to the junior college."

The bell over the door jingled as an older couple wandered in and found seats at the counter.

Jessica watched them enter. "I should get back to work. Nice meeting you." She headed off.

Max rolled her eyes at me. "Smooth."

"Junior college?"

"I had to tell her something. Speak the hell up."

We dug into our breakfast. And for a while, quietly enjoyed our food. I was about half finished, then leaned back and sipped my Sprite. "We should talk about what happened at the lighthouse."

Max jammed a wad of fries into her mouth, then grabbed the ketchup and dumped another puddle onto the middle of her plate.

"Max? Max? Hello. Earth to Max."

She seemed completely engrossed, with her head down, elbows on the table, and a wad of ketchup-drenched fries in her hand. Without moving her head, she looked up at me and continued to chew. "Why?"

"Why? Why what? It's been so long I forgot my question."

"Good. Forget it."

I glared at her.

"We went out on your boat, got caught in a storm, and crashed-landed on Lighthouse Rock. We survived thanks to your amazing boating skills and my ingenuity, and here we are. The end."

I tried to press my point, but she paused her chewing and shot me a look that made me rethink that decision.

We continued to eat in silence. The food hadn't changed, but it'd lost its allure.

"But what about Lester? Suzie? The urns? Don't you think we should talk about that?" I kept my voice low, but I guess I was intense enough that the couple across from us looked over again.

She spoke with her mouth full. "What the fuck are you talking about?"

"I'm talking about the cat, the journal - Hell, you stabbed me in the leg!"

She smiled. "Funny. Stow the bullshit and eat."

"So you don't want to talk about it?"

She kept eating.

"Don't you think—"

"Do you wanna walk home?" She looked past me and made a writing gesture in the air. "Jessica?"

"You haven't finished your fries."

"You haven't stopped being an asshole."

Maybe she really didn't remember. "Okay, okay. Sorry. Just kidding, I guess."

Jessica came over with the check. "Whenever you're ready," she said.

"Thanks," Max said.

Could she have really forgotten everything we'd gone through - the possessions, the fight, how I almost threw her off the rock?

While I was ruminating and sipping my Sprite, she grabbed the check, gave it a quick glance, and slid it in front of me, face-down. "I think this is for you."

I flipped it over. It read:

Thank you.
It's on me.
- Jessie.

She'd written her phone number underneath.

"She got your order right, after all."

I looked around for Jessie, but she'd disappeared.

 "You're welcome," said Max. "Let's go."

We got up from the table and headed outside.

7

RESEARCH

Heavy clouds covered the moon and stars as I stood on the shore, hands in my pockets. The murky water reflected the dim light as soft waves brushed the sand in front of me. Unseen, hidden by the gloom and distance, the dead lighthouse waited - calmly, patiently, hungrily.

A high-pitched, pitiful cry cut the air. I looked down.

On the sand next to me, looking out over the bay, sat a form I'd hoped never to see again. A soft-green glow was the only hint that she wasn't real - or rather, that she wasn't alive. Eartha Kitty - Sam's dead cat - got to her feet, circled around me, then casually stepped out onto the water as if strolling upon the waves was the most natural thing. She moved with them as they gently lifted and fell, then she paused, turned to look back at me, and meowed again. I got the idea that she wanted me to follow. I shivered, but held my ground. She continued her walk out to the sea - out to the damned lighthouse.

I awoke aching and sweaty, feeling as though I'd spent the night fighting off a nightmare attack. I pulled back the covers. The bandage covering the wound in my thigh was stained a deep red. The hole had opened up.

The dream stayed with me as I headed to the bathroom, cleaned and disinfected the wound, then hissing through the sting, applied a new bandage. I got dressed and headed to the kitchen.

After a quick breakfast (Gram always awoke before me and set out cereal or something), I grabbed my crutches and headed out the front door.

As usual, I found her kneeling in the garden, digging into the soft soil with her small spade.

"Bye, Gram," I said, as I set out on my own for the first time since I'd returned.

Shambling along on the crutches gave me time to think. I replayed yesterday's conversation with Max. She'd seemed convinced that the horrible things we'd survived at the lighthouse hadn't happened. I couldn't have dreamed up the whole thing, could I? It all felt surreal and yet hyperreal.

The summer sun on my back, the cool wet mud under my toes, the pain - I didn't think you could feel that stuff in dreams. What was worse, though - infinitely worse - was the bone deep sadness - the loss I shared with Suzie, the little girl whose spirit helped me defeat Lester.

I needed to do some research to prove to Max - and to myself - that it really happened.

The library stood in the center of town - a large, beige Spanish-style building with stucco walls and a red tile roof.

It was a challenge pulling open just one of the massive wooden doors while balancing on crutches.

The fluorescent lights cast everything in a harsh light - the linoleum floors, the shelves, the books, even the people.

I crutched past the librarian's desk, scooping up a pee-wee-golf-sized pencil and a scrap of paper as I went by. The librarian, apparently engrossed in something at her desk, didn't look up. I made my way to the card catalog and began my search.

First, I focused on the lighthouse. I came across the title: *Abandoned: A History of the Santa Carla Lighthouse.*

I copied the book's code and moved on, looking for information about Suzie and her family. I looked under Tod Murders - Lester

Tod - Tod, Lester, etc… It didn't take long before I realized I needed help.

At first, the librarian didn't acknowledge me from behind her red-rimmed reading glasses, perched low on her nose. I cleared my throat.

"Yes?" Her nametag read *Phyllis Lindstrom.* I'd seen quite a few name tags lately.

"Hi, I'm looking for information about a murder that took place in town, back in the fifties."

She didn't reply, so I pressed on. "The family's last name was Tod."

She nodded wrote the name, then typed something into her computer. Phyllis wasn't big on talking.

"It's for a school report." I tried to sound casual. "I'm not into this kind of stuff or anything."

I got the impression she didn't give a damn why I wanted the information. "We have old newspapers saved on microfiche. So, if we don't have a book—no, here we are." She copied the information from the screen, then handed me the paper. Her handwriting was crisp and legible. I thanked her, then headed off in search of the book. It didn't take long to find *Death by the Sea: The Bloody History of Santa Carla - Murder Capital of the World,* written by Charles White. I snatched the book from the shelf and headed toward the nearest empty table.

I scanned the table of contents, and found, close to the bottom of the page; *Tod Family Massacre: Death Among the Redwoods, Page 247.* As I flipped the pages, words and images flipped by in a bleak, black-and-white blur.

I got to page 245. There was the title I'd been looking for, but on the facing page, staring out at me across the decades, was Suzie, her little sister Lizzy, and their mom.

The kids' eyes shone with innocence, their faces bright and smooth and happy, as they sat in their Sunday best. Suzie's hair hung in spiral rivulets. Blond curls danced around her face. Lizzy had straight hair; long and smooth. It glimmered as though it'd been polished and buffed. Their mom's hair was done up like Donna Reed's.

People usually squint when they smile, as if a person's face can't show the whites of the teeth and the eyeballs at the same time. Her eyes were wide open, while her teeth were clenched tight, making her look more pained than happy.

In the back, looming over the girls, stared Lester, his thin hair combed tight to his head, smiling his craggy, pocked-cheek smile. He was cleaner than I'd seen in my vision. No scraggly, uneven beard. His cheeks didn't show the ruddiness of a season in the elements, but it was him just the same. He beamed proudly - the grin of ownership. It was impossible to see that face without tasting bile.

The caption was dated; June, 1954, just a few months before the girls fled—only for Lester to find them, and in just a few savage moments, take away more than their smiles.

Tears dripped onto the page. I hadn't realized I was crying. I wiped them away, but more took their place.

I sat in the uncomfortable wooden chair, in the enforced quiet of that room, and relived that awful scene as if it'd happened to me— because in a sense, it had.

I tried to hang onto the one positive thing about my hellish night in the lighthouse. Those girls were free now. They didn't have to endure Lester's sadistic torments anymore. I'd taken their urns outside, and under the rising sun I'd opened them, releasing their spirits from the confinement they'd endured for so long.

That fact didn't stop the tears though. It didn't erase the awful things they'd gone through. It just meant that for them, it was over.

I flipped the page. Wide, angry eyes stared out from a wild tangle of dark, matted hair and an unkempt beard. He could've been the quintessential Hell's Angel, or a football player with rabies. Below the picture, the caption read in italicized letters, 'William Rickes—executed for the Tod murders, 1964.'

I reread the caption several times. Finally, the words came unbidden from my mouth. "They killed the wrong fucking guy."

The walls felt darker and closer than before. The room felt tight, heavy, too warm. Nervous sweat trickled down my neck.

I had my confirmation. It was real. It had actually happened. Suzy, Lester - the whole thing. I flipped the book over and read the back flap on the dust cover. "Charles White lives and works in Santa Carla, California. He is the Editor-in-chief of the Santa Carla Tattler, In addition, he is the author of…"

The Tattler was a weekly publication you could find stacked in shops all over town. I flipped to the book's copyright page. It was published in 1974, just eight years ago. I felt I was hot on the trail of something. I wasn't sure what, yet.

I grabbed the books and headed over to the newspapers, where I found several copies of The Tattler stuffed in the corner. The address, 114 Seaview, was just a few blocks away. I added it to my pile, and juggling it all, made my awkward way to the door.

"You need to check out," the librarian called out.

"Excuse me?"

"The books?"

I sniffled as I handed them to her, then wiped my eyes with my jacket sleeve as I dug the library card out of my wallet. She paused, seeming to regard me for the first time, and then stuffed everything into a plastic bag.

I thanked her, then hurried out of the building.

8

WHAT THE HELL WAS THAT?

THE SIDEWALKS WERE HEAVY WITH LUNCHTIME TRAFFIC FLOWING IN the opposite direction. I felt like a handicapped salmon, trying to stumble my way upstream.

I'd only traveled about halfway down the block when a brown sedan caught my eye. Nothing special, except it was identical to the car Max's dad drove; a brown, Chevy Nova. I froze, trying to avert my face while trying very hard to think invisible thoughts. Nothing out of place here, just a skinny kid on crutches, petrified like a drunk under a flashlight.

There was no missing his silhouette, the slicked hair, the mustache, the cigar stub protruding from his teeth. His car rolled to the end of the block and turned right. I released the breath I'd been holding, continued on.

A woman caught my attention. It wasn't how she was dressed, or anything like that. It was how she stared at me - square in the eye, as if we knew each other - as if she hated me. She pushed a stroller with a toddler sitting inside, sucking on a red tootsie pop. Her expression morphed into an evil grin. She pivoted and stepped off the sidewalk. Into traffic.

Tires screeched as a blue Volkswagen Beetle skidded to a stop just inches from the stroller. The woman stared straight ahead as she strode into the next lane. A horn blared as a red sedan swerved around her and bashed into the first car's fender. She crossed the yellow centerline. A beige compact weaved right and collided with a car in the next lane. A white pickup truck smashed into the back of it.

Metal crunched, horns screamed, people yelled, the baby bawled, and still she marched forward past the wrecked cars and furious drivers, until she stepped onto the opposite sidewalk. She looked back at me. Her smile had vanished. In its place was that same look as before - naked, hostile loathing. Ignoring the drivers who cursed at her and each other, she held my gaze as she moved down the street and turned the corner, disappearing from view, following the course Detective Morales had taken.

Other folks stopped on the sidewalk, observing the havoc she'd caused. As the crowd grew, I decided to disappear as well.

I continued down the sidewalk and turned left, trying to put the bizarre scene behind me. The shouting and honking continued, fading too slowly into the background.

My body shaking, heart racing, I moved as quickly as I could to put more buildings between me and the scene. Finally, when the chaotic sounds had dimmed into the distance, I allowed myself to pause. I leaned against a glass storefront and breathed as if I'd just sprinted a marathon. I closed my eyes to the world, but all I saw was her face.

Trying to calm my quivering body, I told myself the woman hadn't been looking at me. She'd confused me with someone else. She was crazy. She hadn't just tried to kill herself and her baby as part of a twisted performance for me.

I inhaled, counted four heartbeats, then exhaled slowly, then repeated it again and again. Gradually, my heart slowed, and the pounding in my head eased.

I opened my eyes. The foot traffic was lighter here; even so I realized how I must have looked. I tried to shake it off and continued on my way.

9

A CHANCE MEETING

My destination was on one of the quieter streets just outside the center of town, in a storefront bordered by a used clothing store on one side and a shoe repair shop on the other. The words, *The Santa Carla Tattler*, spelled out in large gold letters, formed a semi-circle in the window. Underneath, it read: Est.1935.

I was familiar with the Tattler, in the way most people were. It was a small, weekly paper, distributed for free, still printed in black-and-white, unlike the big outfits that'd started printing photos in color a couple of years before. It was known mostly for its classified section.

Still feeling shaky, I pushed the door open.

The room was dominated by desks. Each topped by a typewriter and a yellow legal pad. Everything looked old, like it'd been here for years, but too neat. Unused.

It was noon, and the place seemed deserted.

Through a door at the back stepped a man, a little taller than average with more salt than pepper in his hair, and a white button-down shirt with rolled-up sleeves, and a red tie.

He made his way to a coffee maker, picked up the coffee pot, then seemed to notice me.

"Can I help you?" he called out in an easy voice.

"I'm looking for Mr. White."

"You found him. What can I do for you?"

"I saw your name in a book, *Death by the Sea.*

"Always hated that title. Young man, instead of yelling across the room, why don't you come into my office."

"Murder's a heavy subject. This a school project?" he asked as I arrived.

"Not really."

He looked at me sideways, but didn't push further. "And you are?"

"Sam." I held out my hand. "Sam Freman."

He took it. "Nice to meet you, Mr. Freman."

I began talking as he ushered me in. "I guess I'm looking for clarification. I was wondering if you had any more information than you put in your book."

"Almost assuredly." He held the door open, and followed me in.

The room was small. Simple. Photos and awards decorated the wall. He moved behind a cluttered desk and gestured for me to sit in a chair across from him.

"Which case are you talking about?"

"The Tod Murders."

"Up in Boulder Creek. That was way back in forty-seven. Why the interest?"

"Just curious," I lied, then continued. "William Rickes - why did they convict him?"

"I'm sure I covered that in the book. There were other suspects, but the police dismissed them all."

"What about Lester Tod?"

"The father? He couldn't have done it. He was stationed at the old lighthouse."

"But wasn't that around the time the lighthouse crew disappeared?"

"You've done your homework. Yes, that mystery's never been solved. Whatever happened to the Lost Crew of the Lighthouse on Lonely Island?" he asked, wistfully.

"Anyway, why were they so sure Tod didn't do it?"

"Rickes confessed. He walked right into the police station, as calm as you please, and before they could ask a question, he started telling his story. He knew things that no one should've. It was open and shut." He regarded me over his glasses. His look was direct, as was his question. "Why do you think Tod was the man?"

I wasn't ready to answer questions, and I couldn't think of a way around it, so I went with the truth. "I found an old journal. It belonged to the Lighthouse Keeper."

White straightened in his chair. "Calloways' journal? Do you have it?"

"No. I left it there."

"The lighthouse?" He leaned forward. "You're the boy who got stuck out there a few weeks back."

"Yeah. Me and my friend." I felt like I was betraying Max somehow by talking about it.

"So, you found something?"

I nodded.

"Can you tell me about it?"

"It started out pretty boring - a record of how much food they ate, how often they polished the big lens - that sort of thing. But toward the end, he started writing stuff about Lester Tod. How he was hard to get along with. Then things got worse. He got violent. Killed the other keepers. Calloway and Lester got into a fight. Calloway won and… threw Lester off the rock. He managed to write down what happened, but it sounded like he was hurt pretty bad."

"The bodies were never recovered."

"I haven't figured that out yet. Anyway, that wouldn't be in the journal, would it?"

"Good point," said White. "That still doesn't explain why you think he killed his wife."

"Well before that part, he wrote that Lester's wife had gone missing, and Calloway granted him leave to go find her. He came back meaner than before.

Mr. White leaned back in his chair. "Working the crime beat, you get to know the officers. They say you're not supposed to become friends, but sometimes you can't help it." He sipped his coffee as he thought. "Something about the Tod case bothered me. I was just a kid - a cub reporter - not much older than you. The term, serial killer didn't even exist back then and we had two working this area at the same time. It got so people were afraid to go out during the day. The boardwalk all but shut down.

"Anyway, in the middle of all of that, an entire family - massacred. Beaten to death. Those sweet kids... The police had to accept the confession. I mean, Rickes was strong enough, and he had a rap sheet a mile long, but..."

"What?"

"They were settling in for what looked like a long investigation, then Rickes waltzes in one morning and says, polite as can be, 'May I please speak to someone?'

"The police sat him down, and started asking him questions. He gave the right answers. In fact, they said he sounded proud, like he'd really accomplished something by killing those girls. He'd shown them who was in charge."

I was getting chills. "Could someone else have made him confess?"

"You mean like in the movies? I'll tell you there was a lot of pressure to button this thing up. What with the boardwalk being the major draw to this town. No one wants to vacation in the 'Murder Capital of the World,' do they? They wanted this put behind them, and Rickes gave them a way to do that."

We sat for a moment.

"It's funny, though," he said.

"What?"

"For years after that, he begged for a retrial. Claimed he was innocent. Said he didn't know what he was doing when he confessed - right up until they threw the switch." Mr. White looked down into his cup. "It was the first execution I'd attended. Hell of a thing.

As a reporter, I thought I should see the stories through to their end, and it wasn't hard to get access. Like I said, I had friends. Most murderers, by that time, they accept the inevitable. They've had their last meal. They're walked into the chamber, and maybe they have something to say. Maybe not. But Rickes - he fought."

"Did he say why?"

"Why?"

"Why he did it."

"Well, that was the thing. In his confession, he said things like, 'That bitch had it coming to her, she should've known better." That kind of stuff. The detectives suspected it was a rape gone wrong. We all chalked it up to this guy being a lowlife sonofabitch. It was messy. Careless. It happened in the middle of the day. The struggle started inside and moved into the front yard and yet nobody saw."

I saw. I'd witnessed it first hand as if it'd happened to me, thanks to Suzie, the ghost Lester's oldest daughter.

Mr. White took a deep breath then shivered. "Anyway, I should get to work. Has this been helpful?"

"I think so. Thank you for your time."

"Now, I've got a question for you. Did you go to Santa Carla Memorial?"

"I graduated last year."

"There's a football game this Friday. You interested?"

I was taken off-guard. "Thanks, I'm not really into sports."

He didn't move. Didn't say a thing.

Then gears engaged in my brain. "Wait, are you asking me to cover it? As a reporter?"

He smiled. "Call it an audition. It's not much, but I don't have anyone else to do it - times being what they are, we don't really keep a full staff. I could pay you, say, twenty-five dollars."

"Sure!"

Back in '82, you could do a lot with twenty-five bucks.

"Great. Come on back later, and you can get set up with credentials and a camera. You can type, right?"

"Sort of. Thirty-five words a minute."

"That'll be fine. Let me know if you have any more questions about the Tod thing."

"Will do. And thank you."

"Sure thing. Least I can do for the man who might've figured out this town's biggest mystery."

I hobbled out of there feeling lighter than I had in a long time. A job. An actual job. Not at a fast-food place, or at the local pet shop cleaning cages, but doing something kinda cool.

I couldn't wait to get home and tell Gram.

People blurred past. Businesses fell away behind me. I almost giggled as I loped along. So excited. So—

A cat hissed behind me.

I jerked my head toward the sound, searching for the source. All I saw were shops and people. Still moving forward, I turned back around and caught a glimpse of Jessie's face just before I careened into her. She seemed to soar away from me in slow motion, her mouth open wide as if she was singing an opera, her arms reaching out toward me.

She landed bottom-first in the soil of a gardened square next to the street. Bright blue and yellow pansies stared up from the dirt around her with surprised faces.

Her expression matched the flowers'.

I couldn't help it, I laughed. "I'm so sorry." I put both crutches under one arm and offered to help her back up.

She took my hand, then her eyes twinkled and she pulled.

Helpless to stop, I fell forward, landing in the dirt beside her with a jolt.

She laughed harder. "Oh my god, your face."

Her laughter was full of such joy and playfulness.

People stared down at us as they walked by. We laughed harder.

We sat there, next to each other, under a perfect Santa Carla sky, in the moist ground, our butts muddy and damp, with passers-by gaping at us, and we couldn't stop laughing.

She caught her breath. "What was I thinking? Are you okay?"

I waved off her question.

A man wearing an apron raced out of the nearest door. "You kids - what're you doing?"

I grabbed my crutches.

"This isn't a public park!" He yelled.

He tried to wave us off. "Get out of here. Get lost. Shoo!"

Jessie stood up first, wiped her hands on her jeans, then reached down to help me up. She gave me a warning look that said I shouldn't even think of pulling her trick.

I accepted her assistance.

The man saw the flowers, smooshed into our butt-prints in the soil. He grasped his head with both hands. "I-yi. They were just planted."

"I'm Sorry," I said as she pulled me a few steps away. Without thinking, or worrying about the answer, I blurted out, "Hey, would you like to go do something, sometime?"

"Are you asking me out?"

That was when it hit me. "I guess I am." I'd never done that before.

"You guess?" She laughed again.

"I mean, yes. Yes, I'm asking you out."

"Sure."

"…going to call the police," he continued. "You'll be in trouble then."

"Really?" I couldn't believe my ears.

"Uh, sure. Yes. I mean, I'm not busy. Let's go out, please."

"Please?"

"…no respect. What is this city coming to?" The man ranted.

"Yes, please, can we go out?" She seemed flustered. "I'm such an idiot. I'm going to shut up before you change your mind."

I was not going to change my mind.

"When?" She asked.

"How about tonight?"

"I can't. How about Saturday?"

"Saturday. Great! How's four o'clock? We can meet at the Boardwalk."

"It's a date." She said, still smiling. She had a stunning smile.

"Who's going to pay for this?" He literally tugged at the hairs on his head.

"I have to go," she said, releasing my hand.

"Oh yeah, me too." Bullshit. I literally had nothing better to do.

She gave me a quick hug. "Thursday." She backed away, then hurried off.

I stood watching her leave, still feeling the memory of her body against mine, conscious of the huge smile on my face. Finally, the other pedestrians blocked my view, so I only caught glimpses, then she turned the corner and was gone.

"…not kidding. I'll call the police." The shop owner brought me back to myself.

"Mister, I really am sorry." I turned to crutch away.

"Pick up your garbage. I'm not cleaning up after you…"

"I don't have any…" I looked down and saw my bag from the library, still laying in the dirt. "Oh yeah, sorry." I picked it up.

"Don't you come back here." He shouted at my back as I made my way up the street.

What did I care? I had a date!

10

MAX NEEDS HELP

It was later that day, around five-thirty. I'd just settled into the couch, and I Love Lucy was on. Back then, I knew the TV schedule like few other things.

Gram was in the kitchen making dinner, and banged pots and utensils with a rhythm I'd never noticed before. Now, it sounded like home.

Anyway, I was listening to the opening refrains of the Desilu Orchestra when there was a familiar knock on the door.

Since Gram didn't talk, it was up to me to answer.

There stood Max, dressed in kick-your-ass black as usual, but thick ,uneven, black lines ran down from the corners of her eyes. She wiped her nose with her sleeve.

"Can I come in?"

"Of course." I backed away, giving her room. She looked even worse once she stepped into the light. She seemed self-conscious. Beaten. Broken.

"What's up?"

"The bitch threw me out."

"Who?" My response was a reflex, like when someone asks how

you're doing, and you say *fine* without thinking about it. I knew who she was talking about.

She rolled her eyes. "Who do you think?"

"Sorry. What happened?"

"What do you think?"

"Eartha Kitty?" Still the lamest name ever - had been her stepmom's cat. Max had never gotten along with it. Worse, Earth Kitty's main goal to make Max's life hell.

Eartha Kitty was the reason we'd been out on the water. The two of them had developed a warped relationship built on tormenting each other. Max had taken it too far, and the cat ended up dead.

"How did she find out? What did your dad say?"

She was full-on crying now. "Who the fuck knows? I haven't seen him."

Gram stepped into the room and gently took Max into her arms. With her eyes full of concern, she gave me a questioning look.

"Max just got kicked out of her house."

She didn't ask why, or prod for any additional information. She held her for a couple of minutes then guided her into the kitchen, sat her in a chair, retrieved a napkin for her tears, and set a water glass in front of her.

She gestured toward the cabinets, implying that I should set the table for three, and went back to her place in front of the stove.

Before long, Max's tears had quieted and the smells of dinner filled the kitchen. Pot roast – with all the trimmings.

She stepped away from the stove and held out the potato masher for Max

"Awesome." Max got up and started taking her aggressions out on the potatoes. Bits of white starch flew everywhere. Gram placed a comforting hand on her back and pointed at the mess.

"Oh, sorry."

Gram smiled kindly.

Max began again, this time with a little more control. I sat in my chair, feeling pretty much useless until Gram set a loaf of sourdough bread in front of me and a serrated knife.

"Potatoes *and* bread?" We were going overboard with the starch.

Gram pointed at the bread. Her message was clear as always: shut up and get to work. I chuckled and cut six slices. The sounds and the smells of dinner preparation seemed to cleanse the cloud that'd followed Max into the house. Soon we were laughing, almost as if nothing was wrong.

Before long, we sat down with filled plates. There's something about pot roast that means home to me. I've always thought of it as the ultimate comfort food. It tasted amazing, as Gram's meals always did.

We helped ourselves to seconds. But we couldn't fit thirds. We were full.

"Thank you Gram," Max said. "This was amazing." She took a deep breath. "I need to figure out where I'm going to stay tonight."

Gram smacked her hand on the table, pointed at Max, then pointed at the floor. Again, her message was obvious. *You're staying here.*

She held up both hands, stopping Max's protest before it could start. Next, she pointed at the back of the house and then at me.

I laughed. "She's giving you my room."

"I couldn't. Sam's still hurt."

Gram drew her lips together in a thin line. It was settled. We all got up to clear the table.

A little later, as Max and I finished drying and stacking the dishes, Gram left the kitchen, then returned, holding a deck of cards.

When I was little, my family - me, my parents, Grandpa, all crowded around this table, and lost game after game to Gram. It'd been years since we'd played.

The three of us resumed our places. Gram shuffled the cards with a wicked gleam in her eye. The game was Blackjack.

After losing her fourth hand in a row, Max slammed her cards down with mock frustration. "What the fuck, Gram? You hiding cards up your cooch?"

Gram's eyes bulged, and both Max and I burst out laughing.

Gram took pity on us and tended to the final clean-up as we got ready to sleep.

"I can't tell you how much I appreciate this," Max said.

Gram looked at her with her big kind eyes, then put both hands over her heart.

I translated. "It's simple. You're family. Stay as long as you want." Her eyes glistened again, but these weren't sad tears. The truth is, I don't think Max felt like she'd been a part of her own family since her mother died.

We had that in common. We'd both lost parents when we were young.

Max and I headed to my room to get ready for bed. I opened my dresser drawer. "I don't know if you wear pajamas, but you're welcome to mine. I have spares."

Max sat down quietly on the bed. Her shoulders slumped. "She found the collar." She stared at her hand. "I guess she was going through my things and… It didn't seem right throwing it away."

"Did you tell her what happened?"

She shrugged, "She assumes it's my fault, and she's right."

"You didn't do it on purpose."

"I didn't *not* do it on purpose. I mean, obviously I didn't mean to kill the little fucker, but…"

"Try not to think about it. Maybe things will work out."

"How?"

"No idea, but you can stay here as long as you like."

I made my way out to the hallway and opened the linen closet to grab a blanket and a pillow. Suddenly I felt arms around me. I didn't turn around, or say anything. Max isn't good with emotions.

I asked softly, "Is that a chubby?"

She laughed quietly, and sniffed. "Way to make it awkward," She released her hug, turned around, and headed back into my room. "Night."

11

A REALIZATION

"Sam. For fuck's sake, wake up." I awoke to Max whisper-shouting my name, frantically shaking me by the shoulder. It was still dark, but I could make out her form above me, and there was no mistaking that voice. "What's this?"

"What's what?" I could see she was holding something rectangular.

"This." She switched on the light. The brilliance washed out the rest of the world. "Hey."

"What the fuck is this?" Her voice sounded urgent, bordering on panic. Through squinted eyes, I could see the shine of wetness on her cheeks.

I was now fully awake. I sat up. She set something heavy in my lap.

I lifted it. "It's a book." It was in fact, one of the books I'd picked up from the library.

"I know it's a book, dipshit. What's this?" She opened it to the page I'd saved with the paper scrap and tapped the picture of the Tod family.

My stomach clenched. "That's Suzie, and—"

"Lester." She interjected. "I know it's Lester. But how the fuck do I know?"

"He killed them."

"Dammit, I know what he did, but how do I know?" she asked in a louder voice, cracking from the force of emotion behind it.

I scooted over so she could sit next to me as I tried to organize my thoughts. "This might take a while."

I recounted the events in the lighthouse as I remembered them.

"So, you're seeing the ghost of that goddamned cat?"

"Not so much, anymore. And for the record, I think it's Lester we need to focus on."

"That little shit."

"Who?"

"That fucking cat. It just had to get back at me."

I couldn't help myself. I smiled. "So, you think this is Eartha Kitty's fault?" I decided not to argue the point. "How're you feeling?"

Her eyes teared up again. "Like I've been fucking violated. How about you?"

"Oh, you know - the usual. Panic attacks, nightmares." As hard as it had been for me, I'd had a couple of weeks to process. She was getting hit with this for the first time, and apparently, got it all in one shot.

Her tears had stopped. She took a moment to collect her thoughts. "He kept showing me the things he was going to make me do to you, and the stuff he was going to do to me, after. I think he got off on showing me how weak I was."

"You kept - that is, He kept telling me how he wasn't letting me take his family."

"And you did it, anyway." She sounded impressed.

I closed the book. "You saw things from his point of view. Suzy showed what it was like for her."

"So, is it over?" she needed reassurance. She wanted to know that everything was okay.

I shrugged. "I'm pretty sure Suzy the others moved on, whatever that means."

"What about Lester."

I shrugged again. "Maybe he did. Maybe we left him in the lighthouse. I don't know."

"So, we're supposed go on, like everything's okay?"

"That's what I've been doing. What choice do we have?"

"I don't know. Call an exorcist?" She smiled.

"Maybe, now that you remember too, we can come up with a strategy together."

She nodded quietly.

We were quiet for a few moments. Then I realized there was something I needed to say "By the way, I'm sorry."

"For what?"

"For everything. For almost getting us killed in that storm. For the lighthouse. For every-fucking-thing!"

"Why do you keep saying that? It wasn't your fault."

"Yes, it was. We never should've been out there. My Grampa taught me that—"

"You were trying to help me." She took my hand.

I shook my head, pretty sure I'd always feel guilty. "It's still dark out. You wanna try to get some sleep?"

"Are you kidding? I'm never sleeping again."

I laughed, picked up the TV remote and switched it on. "Me neither."

12

A CRY IN THE NIGHT

It was game night: With a backpack slung over my shoulders, and crutches under my arms, I walked into my old high school stadium.

In the four years I'd attended this school, I'd never once gone to a football game - partially because I hated sports, but also because Kavenaugh was the high school quarterback. He and his cronies owned the place, and it would've been like walking into his own house.

It occurred to me that there was a chance he'd show up to this game. The old fear raised its head. Maybe he'd want to relive the old days with his buddies by pounding me into the stands or "pantsing" me in the end zone. I knew it wasn't likely, but that's how my mind works.

I pushed those thoughts aside. I had a job to do. With my credentials hanging around my neck, I felt as if I had a purpose - something to prove.

I'd arrived about an hour before kick-off. Maybe that was overkill, but I really didn't know what I was doing.

A few adults hovered around the snack shack, while a couple others organized the candy and drink cups inside. I caught a snippet of their conversation. "Does it seem strange that we're going ahead with the game?" said one of the women.

A man replied, "Would you rather we put our lives on hold? The girl's probably fine."

I passed a light pole with a xeroxed flier taped to it. A stunning girl wearing a cheerleader's outfit smiled from the paper. Her name was Christine Dunn, *Missing* it said, with a five hundred dollar reward offered for information. I remembered her from school. She was a gifted student, with friends. Who would want to run away from that? She was popular, and always seemed nice. I'd never spoken to her, but then, I hardly talked to anyone in school, let alone, gorgeous cheerleaders.

The stands were empty. I found a seat down front, near the 50-yard line.

I pulled out a spiral notebook leftover from my days as a student and flipped past the few pages of old chemistry notes, then folded it over. I wrote 'Football Game' at the top of the first blank page. *Santa Carla Mustangs vs. ?* I didn't know who the opposing team was. I assumed I'd figure it out.

The sky, all pink fire, spread out above me. The stadium lights switched on, and I squinted against them as I stared at the neon clouds beyond.

A light breeze brought a chill, so I zipped up my jacket and looked around for any details I could include in my article.

An elderly couple carrying blankets and seat cushions climbed past and sat in the row behind me.

I didn't see anything worth noting, so I set the notebook aside and pulled out the camera case. It was a standard Canon SLR, just like the ones I'd used in my photography class. I made sure it contained film, then cleaned the lens, and fired off a couple of test shots. I now had absolutely nothing to do but wait for the game to start.

Slowly, the stands filled up.

The mood was somber, quiet, tense.

"Her poor parents."

"Do the police have any idea…?"

"How long has she been missing?"

"Would it be better if she was dead?"

Comments and questions surrounded me.

Having recently become intimately familiar with death, I couldn't help but put myself in her position. I understood fearing you'd never see your loved ones again.

The elderly woman behind me spoke in a loud whisper. "Maybe we should've stayed home."

"Nonsense," said the old man. "The house is like a mausoleum - better to get out and see people." There was a pause. "Come on, now. Brave face."

The sadness exuded from them like stink from a corpse.

A middle-aged couple passing me, stopped to greet the old couple. "Tom, Maureen - how're you holding up?"

"As well as we can," Tom replied.

My instinct was to sit quietly and pretend to take notes. But it felt ghoulish to listen in on their conversation. They obviously knew the missing girl. I thought about changing seats. The couple moved on, and instead of leaving, I swiveled around to face them. "I'm sorry for intruding. Do you know the missing girl?"

They were sitting close together, a shared blanket covered their laps. The old man wrapped his arm around his wife.

"Christine's our granddaughter," Maureen said.

"I'm sorry." I didn't know what else to say.

"Do you know her?" she asked.

I remembered seeing her in the hallway, walking with her friends, dressed in their red and white uniforms, cradling their books, laughing casually. Completely unaware that she owned the place.

She'd never noticed me. Why would she? I would've been conspicuous in the way I tried to hide, hugging the lockers to stay out of the way.

Sure I knew her - the way you know the sun or the moon. You see them every day, but you're locked in orbit, never close enough to touch, yet still they affect your world.

She'd never directed her radiance on me, but I couldn't help but be dazzled.

"I didn't. She seemed nice," I said.

He smiled, then after a moment blurted out, "The Wildcats."

"Pardon?"

"Your notebook. They're playing the Watsonville Wildcats."

"Oh, thank you." I scribbled the information.

"Tom, they're our biggest rivals, she should be here." said Maureen.

"She's probably fine, dear."

"If she was okay, she'd be here." Maureen turned to me. "She loved being a cheerleader. She had such good friends. All the boys liked her."

What was I supposed to say, *It'll be okay? It'll all work out?* Those were lies you tell people so their own pain won't make you uncomfortable. I noticed she'd referred to Christine in the past tense.

I settled for, "I really hope she comes home soon."

Maureen wasn't comforted. "Can we go?" She said to Tom.

Quietly they gathered their things and stood up. She pointed at my notebook. "You be sure to say how much we love her." They headed toward the exit.

I simply nodded, then I put my pen to the paper and started jotting what I remembered from our conversation.

I felt someone standing next to me. Thinking the old couple had returned, I looked up and gazed into a pair of tragically beautiful, blue eyes. Christine Dunn stared back, unblinking. Our gazes locked. I couldn't look away. She laid her hand on my shoulder.

The crowd, the stadium, everything flashed away.

My limbs felt longer, more supple. My hair lay across the back of my neck.

My feet were crammed into hard leather shoes. They jammed my toes together, and required balance to negotiate the high, narrow heel.

I could only watch - a spectator in someone else's body - an incredibly intimate view of a show I wanted no part of.

Christine walked down a lonely street at night, wearing a short dress. A chill wind blew across her bare legs. Were they my legs now? I felt unbalanced, maybe a little drunk. Her mouth was dry and sticky. She'd been out with a friend, but was alone now.

She wandered through downtown Santa Carla, lost with no idea where she'd left her car - a pretty red Celica her parents had bought as a reward for getting good grades.

Her breath came in quick, short bursts. Steam escaped her mouth to join with the fog.

The night had been her friend, Becca's idea. She'd bought a couple of fake IDs, and had wanted to try them out. She loved taking risks.

It sounded fun when she'd explained her plan: pretend to be grown-ups, have a few drinks, and then go back to her house and spend the night—like Christine had told her parents she was doing.

"Fuck you, Becca," she called out. The fog absorbed her voice, muffled it.

The bar's fluorescent lights had been dim and garish at the same time, giving everyone an unnatural, pink hue.

Some unwashed, bearded old pervert bought the girls tequila shots. Then they cut out to search for - as Becca put it - better hunting - a new place she'd heard about. They got lost, but after retracing their steps, eventually found it.

Becca had this strange ability to make the stupidest things seem fun. By stupid, I mean scary. She made you feel everything would turn out okay, and until now, everything had.

Tonight though, she'd disappeared with some guy, and left Chrissy alone.

The second place - louder than the first - had a jukebox playing hard rock: Blue Oyster Cult, The Scorpions, Black Sabbath, and a bunch of other bands she couldn't stand. A guy with slick hair and a shiny gray suit bought them drinks. He didn't ask if they wanted them. He just called the bartender by name, and said 'Two more,' and pointed to them. A slight improvement over the bearded degenerate from earlier. But only slight. It wasn't long before he and Becca started flirting.

Becca said she had to go to the ladies' room, and gave Chrissy a look that demanded she go with her.

She gushed over him as we stood in front of the mirror, applying fresh coats of lipstick. She told me she was taking him outside.

She caught Chrissy's annoyed look. "Lighten up. Find someone. Have some fun for a change."

Chrissy sat by herself for another hour. It seemed longer. Guys came up and tried to talk, but without Becca, she didn't know what to say, and didn't want to try.

Finally, the bartender unplugged the jukebox. "Last call, ladies."

She'd waited long enough. She shrugged into her fringed leather jacket, grabbed her purse, and stepped out through the back door. The frigid night bit at her bare legs. Just a few scattered cars sat wet and lonely in the parking lot. She crept past them, peering through the windshields, trying to see movement, silhouettes, signs of life. There were none.

"Fuck you, Becca," she whispered.

Her uneasiness rising, she headed back into the bar. At least it was warmer and better lit. She hadn't even sat down when someone grabbed her arm. "Hey baby, looks like I'm the best you're gonna do."

"Oh no, I'm looking for my…" His grip tightened. She looked around for help. The place had emptied.

She tugged. He wouldn't let go. "I know a place that's open a few more hours," he slurred. He was missing one of his top teeth. She glanced at the door, praying that Becca would sweep in and get her out of there.

The bartender came in from the back with a white towel hanging off his shoulder. "Okay, you two. Time to call it a night."

The guy pulled Christine closer. She smelled whiskey on his breath, and something worse. "Come on, let's—"

A shadow loomed over them. "Ben, the lady isn't interested. Let her go," said the bartender.

"We're just getting to know one another."

The bartender rested his hand on Ben's shoulder and leaned in close. "The lady knows you well enough. Go home."

Ben released her arm like he'd been scorched. "Fine."

Defeated, he stumbled back, and mumbling to himself, stepped out the back door and into the night.

"Thank you," she said gratefully.

"Where's your friend?"

"I don't know. She left with some guy. Can I wait for her?"

"If you do it outside."

Her eyes shot to the door through which Ben had just passed.

"She's a big girl. You okay to drive?"

"Yeah, I'm fine." Chrissy left out the part about how she'd forgotten where she'd parked. She didn't want him to think she was just a dumb kid. Seeing no alternative, she headed toward the front door, the opposite way Ben had chosen, and stepped back out into the gloom. She'd only gone a few steps when the bar's lights switched off behind her.

She was completely alone, on the street, in the dark.

She started walking, trying to get her bearings. The streetlights illuminated globes of moisture around them, but not much else. The moon hid above the thick fog. She passed a gloomy row of shops: a secretarial firm, an office, a seedy little Mexican restaurant. Everything was closed. Shadowed. Dead.

She'd grown up in Santa Carla, She knew these streets, but the dark and the fog and the liquor and the fear combined to make everything look alien, unfamiliar.

I wanted to tell her, *Your car's in the parking lot on 2nd street, just a couple blocks away.* I saw it in her memory. But I had no voice, no way to reach her.

Her eyes darted in every direction as she walked, desperately searching for something familiar. Just one landmark would be enough.

Her shadow stretched and grew more distinct in front of her as a car, its motor rumbling low and menacing, approached slowly from behind. It pulled up next to her. She made a point to not look at it.

The motor growled and her fear climbed along with it.

"Hey, sweetie," a voice called from inside, "need a ride?"

"Yeah," giggled another, in a higher pitch. "You need a ride?"

She clutched her bag tight and walked faster.

"Hey, don't be a bitch."

"Yeah, be nice." Another giggle.

She glanced over involuntarily. It was a big car - beefy - an old Camaro painted deep red, with over-sized tires. She couldn't see features inside. Then a cigarette glowed in the dark, illuminating the lower half of a shadowed face. Smoke billowed out of the window into the night.

"You're looking fine. Come on, we can have fun."

They weren't going away.

She had an idea. Maybe she'd seen it in a movie or a TV show - "Police Woman" or something. Anyway, It was really lame, but it was all she could think of. With her heart beating fast and loud, she stopped and faced them, fighting the urge to run. Instead, she smiled as best she could. "You boys want to party?"

"You know it."

"Haha, yeah, you know it."

She opened her purse, slow, deliberate, obvious, then reached her hand in – again, slowly, trying to will it steady. "Let's play," she said as she pulled out her hand and pointed a silver barrel into the dark cab, aiming for where the driver should be. "Wanna do shots?"

"Wait. What the fuck?"

"Dude, go. Go!"

The engine roared, tires squealed. The car raced off into the night.

She stood, shaking in her painful shoes. Her purse quivered as she dropped the lipstick back into it. She turned and ran the other way, to the end of the block, and turned right, so she wouldn't be anywhere near the same spot when they figured out that she'd bluffed them.

I felt everything that she felt, shared every thought. The longer I was part of her, the more intimately our minds connected. It became harder to think of myself as Sam as I experienced life through her senses.

That wasn't the only confusing part of it though, because mixed in with her emotions and her thoughts were my own - muted. Somehow blunted by the fact that I was no longer in my own body.

What's worse, I couldn't do anything to help.

Have you ever watched nature shows, like Wild Kingdom, or those National Geographic specials? Sometimes, when wolves go hunting, they let the puppies take the first crack - like some kind of twisted, learning exercise. They're sloppy, treating the hunt like play, and almost always, the intended prey escapes.

That's how it felt. The sloppy young predators had taken their shot, but because they were stupid, Christine got away. What if — chills ran up her spine as I wondered this—what if now that she'd escaped the novices, it was the alpha's turn?

She glanced at her dim reflection in a window as she walked past, thinking that if someone followed silently behind, she might see them, and, at the same time, prayed she saw nothing.

She continued on her way for hours it seemed, her purse still clutched to her chest, keeping one eye on her reflection of the windows we passed, while trying to see all around her at once, desperate to spot anything that looked familiar.

"Finally!" She exclaimed, as just ahead, across the street, stood a building significantly larger than the rest. Roughly three stories tall, it took up an entire block. As Chrissy approached, she made out the name painted on the wall, *Ben Franklin's Fine Fashions*.

"Fine fashion - as if," Becca had said.

"As if," Chrissy parroted into the dark. "Fuck you, Becca." She picked up her pace, her fear growing along with her hope. Wolves usually waited at the watering hole, didn't they?

Hope gave her the ability to think beyond her immediate circumstances. Once she was in her car, where should she go? Should she drive around looking for Becca? She promised herself that she'd return to the bar and check the parking lot again. Maybe she'd be there. Maybe she was waiting there already. The slimy guy with the greasy ponytail had probably brought her back out of the kindness of his heart - a perfectly reasonable thing to expect. Sure.

What if she wasn't there? Should she go back to Becca's house? What if she wasn't there either?

No - Chrissy decided - she'd be okay. Becca was always okay.

"Fuck you, Becca," she whispered.

She crossed in front of Ben Franklin's now. We just had to get around the corner, and into the lot behind.

She heard a scratch. A shoe scuff or something. Was it behind her? Ahead?

She picked up her pace again. Her heel caught on a raised bump on the sidewalk and she stumbled. Somehow, she stayed on her feet and hurried on.

She passed *Ben Franklin's* and turned the corner. The parking lot lay just ahead. She spotted her Celica sitting by itself in the dark, beneath a broken street light.

Her keys jingled as she lifted them out of her purse. She selected the correct one without looking, and held it ready. Her heart beating fast and loud, she ran the last, few feet to her car. With nervous fingers, she fumbled, gouging the paint around the lock. Finally, the key slid in and turned. Inside, the stem popped up with a comforting click. She pulled the handle and swung the door open.

She ducked her head and lowered herself in, exhaling relief as she pulled the door.

It wouldn't close. Something blocked it.

A shadow filled the opening. He grabbed her arm. Light and pain exploded in her cheek as he struck her face. A hand grasped the back of her head and slammed it forward, bashing her into the steering wheel, breaking her nose with a loud crack. She cried out, her vision glazed with tears. She wrapped her free arm around the wheel and tried to wrench the other arm away from his grasp. He wadded her hair in his hand and wrenched her head back, then threw it into the wheel again, then again, and again, and again.

He pulled her arm, trying to pry her from the car. She helped on tight.

He got his arm around her neck and twisted his body. With her head swimming in pain and confusion, the wheel slid out of her grip and he dragged her out into the night.

Chrissy screamed.

He was wide, burly, barrel-chested—and so damned strong.

Chrissy's knees scraped the asphalt as he dragged her further from the car, her legs flailing behind, her screams desperate. Feral.

He let go, and she fell to the ground, fighting for air. The keys dug into her palm. The keys!

Grasping her hair again, he wrenched her head back. She glimpsed his face - a blur of rough features against the foggy night. Mottled skin, slicked hair, narrowed eyes. He stank of sweat. His breath was rancid.

She lashed out. The key's metal teeth missed his eye, but dug into his cheek and raked down. He stumbled back, his hand flying to his face. Blood glistened between his fingers.

She kicked at his shin, then rolled over onto her stomach and crawled back toward her car. Refuge. Safety.

He kicked her in the side. It forced the breath out of her, but she continued to crawl. He stomped on her back. Something cracked. Everything was agony. Still, she dragged herself forward.

He flipped her over. She tried to scramble. He lifted his foot over her face. Time stopped for a moment. It was a plain shoe. Black, with laces. A hole worn in the bottom, just under the big toe. It grew larger as it crashed down. Everything went dark.

I flooded back into myself in a rush. The air was lighter, lit by towers high above. Movement surrounded me as the crowd gathered their things and made their way down the bleachers. Below, the athletes moped off the field, their heads bowed. There was no excited murmur. No joy. The game was over. I'd missed it. The crowd shuffled out quietly as if leaving a funeral.

I wiped tears from my cheeks. To my left stood a man holding a wadded blanket. Behind him, a line had formed, apparently waiting for me to get up.

I collected the camera and notebook and jammed them into my backpack, zipped it closed, then I grabbed the crutches and stood up, disoriented by the sudden change.

"What happened?" I asked.

"We lost," he replied. His face was as bleak as my mood. It didn't feel right to ask anything else. It didn't seem to matter.

I was still halfway in the vision, marinating in the fear and grief of living through another death.

It seeped in slowly. I was back. Unhurt. Alive.

I stepped onto the stairs and joined the crowd - alone in the knowledge that Christine Dunn was dead.

13

PONDERINGS

Instead of going straight home, I wandered, trying to deal with what I'd seen. It was like my experience with Suzy - too real to be a dream, too fucked up to believe.

Why had Chrissy reached out to me? She had so many friends who missed her. She had a family. I hadn't spoken to her once back in school. I never had the guts.

I needed to tell someone, but who? What would I tell them? They'd ask me how I knew. I didn't - oh God - didn't even know what'd happened to her body. I hadn't seen the face of her attacker. It was too dark. Too savage.

All I knew was she was dead. I couldn't help find her body or her attacker.

Still, I had a responsibility, didn't I? People needed to know what happened. Was that what she was asking me to do?

Max would understand, but what would I say to Gram?

By the time I got home, the house was quiet.

I was sure when I laid down on the couch, I wouldn't sleep. For a long time I was right, as Chrissy's murder replayed itself in my head. I guess finally, I drifted off.

There was a flash, and I'd returned to the beach. The night air blew through my jacket. This time, the sky was clear. The moon and stars shone down onto the water, highlighting the crests of the waves.

I felt a presence and looked down. Beside me, sat Earth Kitty, simply staring out, away from shore. It meowed without breaking its gaze.

The lighthouse seemed larger, somehow closer to shore - maybe just a couple hundred yards away.

She stepped onto the water, took a few steps, then looked back at me. Her meow was more urgent this time. She stared a moment, then turned back toward the lighthouse as thunder rumbled in the distance.

14

THE DATE

Tonight was my date with Jessie. I had all day to get ready, but decided to go against my nature and get dressed early. If Gram had been home I would've asked for her input. Still, how hard could it be? Pants, shirt, shoes, some underwear underneath all that, and done. Hell, I'd been dressing myself for years. I had this.

With a little less than an hour still to go, I was confident I had everything under control.

Max returned early from work to find me sitting on the couch, watching TV. "You're going out like that?"

I thought I looked fine - better than fine - almost good. "Why? What's wrong?"

She smiled and shook her head. "I mean, if that's the best you can do."

"Seriously, what's wrong with my clothes?"

"Nothing. You look okay, I suppose."

"Just okay?" I said as I hurried back to the bathroom.

I stood in front of the mirror. What stared back wasn't a surprise, but it was unimpressive. Now that I analyzed it, it was downright sad.

"Shit!" I thought I was ready. I rushed into my room. Now, I was pressed for time. I slammed the closet door open. "Where are my shirts?" The room brightened suddenly. Max had flicked the light switch.

"Are you okay?"

"I thought I was." I took a breath. "I need a shirt." I turned back toward the closet. It was filled with clothes but I needed a shirt. "Where are my shirts?"

Smirking, she sauntered over and pulled one down from among the bunch hanging right in front of me, holding it out with a concerned look on her face.

"Thank you." I snatched it out of her hand, put it back and then grabbed another, then I put that back and pulled out yet another. I put that back and stared. Finally, I paused, and selected the one that seemed best - the one Max pulled out originally. I tore off the shirt I was wearing, pulled the new one over my arms, and buttoned it up.

I tore into the bathroom to check the mirror. Something was wrong. The collar looked wonky, one side higher than the other. "What the hell?" I said in a panic.

"Breathe, hysterical boy," she stepped forward and unbuttoned my shirt.

"What're you...?"

"I said breathe." She smiled, obviously enjoying this.

I took deep breaths as she re-buttoned it, then turned me around. My reflection looked less wrong.

"Thank you." I grabbed my toothbrush, and stared at it a moment. What was this for, I wondered?

She placed the toothpaste in my hand. I squeezed out some out, stuffed the brush in my mouth then reached for my comb. I ran it through my hair while I scrubbed my teeth. This wasn't going well.

Max smiled. "What the fuck are you doing?" she laughed.

I stopped. One thing at a time, I told myself. I exhaled, set down the comb, finished with my teeth, then fixed my hair.

I headed back into my room, looked at myself in the mirror, then looked over at Max. "Okay?"

"Sure." She smiled, then we headed out.

"By the way, where's Gram?" She asked.

"Shit. Gram!" I grabbed the pencil and paper that sat next to the phone.

Gram, Don't plan on me for dinner. I have a date!

I placed the note on top of the phone so she wouldn't miss it, dashed into my room to grab my house key, then followed Max out the door.

"Do you have money?" Max asked.

"For...?"

"Your date. Is she paying for you? Hello?"

"Shit." I unlocked the door and ran inside, reached into my dresser, and grabbed my allowance envelope from the top drawer. It was empty.

"Max?" I yelled.

"What?" she replied.

I jumped.

She was standing in the doorway.

"Can I borrow some money?"

She rolled her eyes. "How much do you need?" She reached into her pocket and pulled out some bills.

"Twenty dollars would be great."

She peeled off forty and held it out for me.

I stuffed them in my pocket. "You're awesome."

We started for the door.

"Shit. My jacket." I stepped back into my room and scooped it off the back of my desk chair, then came back out.

"Shoes?"

"Crap." Back into my room I went, and stepped into them.

"Key?"

I caught the door just before it closed, ran back to my room. It wasn't on the dresser. It wasn't on my desk. I patted my jeans. It wasn't in my front pocket.

I jammed my hands into my back pockets, it wasn't there either. I turned around. I checked my jacket. Nothing. Where was it?

I caught my reflection in the mirror. Everything seemed in place.

Then I saw the glint of metal in my hand. "Fuck me!" I dropped it into my pocket.

I almost charged out, when I caught site of my crutches leaning against the wall. I grabbed them and followed her outside. "Don't say a word."

Laughing, she started the car.

"Thank you for driving." I said as we drove off.

"Don't mention it. Just do me a favor."

""What's that?'

"Try to not be such a virgin."

"What does that mean?"

She laughed. "I'm just kidding."

"I need to talk to you about something."

"I don't know shit about condoms or blowjobs."

"No, something happened at the game yesterday."

"Something bad, I assume?"

I nodded.

"Tell you what, you've got a date you need to be up for, and I really don't want to hear anything heavy right after work. How about if we save it for tomorrow."

She had a point, as just then we arrived.

Standing next to the entrance to the Boardwalk, Jessie looked stunning, effortless in a yellow t-shirt and a pink cardigan, with her hair pulled back in a simple hairband.

In the middle of November, she looked like spring.

"Thanks, Max." I jumped out, grabbed my crutches from the truck bed and started across the street.

"You kids have a good time," she yelled.

"Thank you."

"Don't stay out too late."

I smiled. This was the price for the ride.

"Thanks, Max." I waved without turning back.

"Hi," I said to Jessie.

"Hi yourself," she said.

"Play nice," Max yelled. "Sam, remember your manners."

I waved.

She swung into an illegal u-turn, so she was on our side of the street and let loose with her parting shot. "Use a condom."

I shook my head.

Giggling, Jessie slipped her arm through mine and together, we walked through the entrance with all the other kids, both young and old.

The Boardwalk is a hub for our town. When tourists visit, it's usually the first place they go. A permanent carnival by the sea.

It's always an interesting cross-section; families on holiday, older kids, dropped off so that mom and dad could enjoy some one-on-one time. Local kids hanging out.

To round it out, we had hookers, bikers selling drugs, and the occasional stray dog.

Yep, something for everyone.

"So, what do you want to do first?" She asked. She had to yell to be heard over the music screeching from the tilt-a-whirl, spinning just inside the entrance.

"It's up to you."

"How about the roller coaster!"

"Great," I said. Inside I shuddered. I hate roller coasters. So many things about them make me uncomfortable. One - they're filled with screaming people. Two - they go fast. I hate how they jerk me around. Three - and this is the important part - they go up high. I'm not good with heights. I hate heights. I fear heights. Heights are not my friend.

So, we got in line for the roller coaster. Her arm still looped with mine. I think that if she'd wanted to dive off the top of the ferris wheel, I'd have done it if she promised to not let go.

The line moved quickly. The place was busy, but not crowded like it got on summer weekends.

The music blasted us from every side at once. Talking was out of the question.

We passed a plywood pelican. His voice bubble read: *You must be this tall to ride the Stardust Rollercoaster.*"

My heart raced. My stomach tightened. You'll be okay, I told myself. This is fun. People do it all the time. No one's been killed on a roller coaster in years, right? I didn't know, but I hoped it'd been a long time.

I handed my crutches to the high school kid running the attraction, and eased myself into the hard, plastic seat.

Of course we were in the front car. Terrific. The operator made sure we all pulled the safety bars down tight across our laps. "Keep your hands inside the car at all times," he warned. He pushed a lever forward, and we lurched into motion. My gut lurched too, as slowly, the mechanism pulled us up and away from the crowd and the ground and safety.

Jessie's eyes were wide and bright. Her smile, effervescent. For a few seconds I forgot this was something I was afraid of. I couldn't help but smile back.

She put her hands up in the air. I did the same.

Slowly, the coaster click-clacked to the top. We could see the mass of people down on the boardwalk, walking in all directions, with groups of children weaving their way through. As we climbed higher, I could see the beach stretched out beyond. A sandy ribbon between the boardwalk and the water. The bay sparkled under the fiery pink sky of the setting sun. Anchored boats danced lightly on the incoming waves. Beyond, the water changed its texture, peppered with larger waves. I could almost ignore that, in the distance, just outside the bay, stood the lighthouse.

It was cooler up here. The breeze blew across my face and gently lifted the few chestnut hairs that escaped Jessie's ponytail.

The ground seemed so far away now, and I asked myself, shouldn't I be afraid?

Instead, I looked at Jessie, the sunlight on her hair, the joy on her face. Was that a touch of fear in her eyes? No. Not actual fear, just the exciting spice that seasons activities like this and makes them fun.

Just look at Jessie, I thought. You'll be fine.

I thought she was pretty when we met her at The Wave, but here, up high above the crowd, her hair shining in the magic sunlight. She was stunning.

Why would she pick me? I was a dork. A geek. A loner. I wasn't the guy who got girls. I was the guy who got beat up by the guys who got girls.

The coaster reached the top. There was a loud "chunk". Alarmed, I grabbed at the bar in front of me, but Jessie kept her hands raised high in the air. Now free, we glided slowly forward, the car following the tracks in a gentle turn. We seemed to hang in mid-air. Out over the sea, the setting sun hovered just inches it seemed, above the water.

Jessie screamed. I ripped my attention back to the here and now as the tracks disappeared in front of us. She grabbed my hand and hoisted it above us, and down we plunged toward the ground.

The rattle filled my ears. Air blasted my face. Jessie screamed again. I trained my eyes on the track, trying to anticipate the direction the car would go.

We banked a sharp turn, and then another. She giggled. I did my best to imitate her.

She held fast to my hand, keeping it aloft. There was no way I was letting go for something as silly as saving my life.

I glanced at the wooden struts as they blurred by. How strong could they be after all this time? The boardwalk was old. Over a hundred years old. How old was the roller coaster? It looked ancient. Were those timbers solid, or rotted with age and salt air? People checked those things, right?

The car shot up a short incline, and then just as quickly dove again. We were weightless for a split second. The safety bar dug into my injured leg, then our butts hit the seat, and we jetted into another sharp turn, then another in the opposite direction. One moment we were free of gravity, and the next, we were pushed down into the seat. The car heaved and jumped and spun, like a bronco trying to buck us off, but with our hands high in the air, somehow, our butts clung to the seat. We swerved a final time, slowed suddenly, then jerked to a stop back where we'd started. Safe, if a little shook up. The bar lifted, and the kid instructed us to watch our step and to enjoy our time at Santa Carla's Beach and Boardwalk.

"Let's do that again." She said as I grabbed my crutches.

"Cool!" I decided that either this date was going to kill me, or I was going to learn to like roller coasters.

We rode it three times, then the tilt-a-whirl, and a few more rides. Finally, we paused for a soft-serve. She held both cones as we descended the short flight of stares onto the beach to escape the cacophony of the carnival for a while. She traded one cone for one of my crutches.

Leaving the flashing lights behind, we gazed out at the stars spread out above.

The music faded a little. No longer fighting for attention, it became more like a soundtrack. We passed a couple lying on blankets. Their boom box played the final refrain of Journeys' "Still They Ride". I didn't really know what the song was about, I always pictured bikers ablaze with fire, flying through the night sky. The song ended and Don't Fear the Reaper followed.

Distracted by the music, I paused. I'd always liked the song, but after my adventure in the lighthouse, the lyrics seemed poignant. Relevant. Maybe too close to home.

Jessie bumped me with her shoulder, holding the ice cream up so I could take a lick. "You okay?"

I nodded, ice cream dripped down my chin. She wiped it with the sleeve of her sweater.

I felt almost giddy. How was I so lucky?

She cocked her head. "What?"

I caught myself staring. "Nothing," I stammered.

The stars glittered intense and bright over the water. She turned toward the sea.

Pretending she held an imaginary camera, "Click. Kodak moment." The sound of the waves lapping the shore replaced the music and we shared the spectacle nature put on for us. She rested her head on my shoulder, as she licked her ice cream.

I leaned my head on hers. Could it really be this easy? Shut up and enjoy, I told myself, trying to drown out the annoying voice in my head that never seemed to stop.

She turned to face me, her gaze darted over my head.

I turned as the Ferris wheel blazed in neon life, outshining the stars under the black sky.

"Wow." The word escaped my lips.

"Wow." She echoed.

We watched it spin for a moment, then as one, we turned back toward the water, but we paused halfway, facing each other, and without thinking or stressing or anything else, we kissed. It was soft and sweet and cool from the ice cream. We lingered for just a moment, and then turned back toward nature's show, put on just for us. Eddy Money's "Two tickets to paradise" played in the air.

God, what an amazing night.

Slowly, we strolled across the beach toward the wharf, then we found an empty bench, and sat to watch people go by.

"I'm just working at The Wave part-time while I take classes at Cabrillo." She said in answer to my question. "Charlie was so nice when I applied, and he's willing to work around school. How about you?"

"Me? I like Charlie fine."

"No, goofball. What do you want to be when you grow up?"

Across from us, a beach bum shuffled by and reached into the garbage can, apparently looking for his evening meal.

I nodded in his direction. "Life goals."

She slapped my arm playfully. "Be nice."

"Sorry. Actually, I just got a job at The Tattler - sort of."

"Sort of?"

I told her I'd covered the game. I didn't go into details.

She raised her eyebrows. "A journalist?"

"Maybe. At least I don't have to wear a paper hat."

She rolled her eyes. "How'd you get it?"

"It's kind of a long story, I guess." I wasn't ready to tell her about my adventure in the lighthouse yet.

She seemed satisfied with that for now. Again, she rested her head on my shoulder, and we sat there like an old married couple watching the tourists; kids, hopped up on sugar, ran from one gift shop to another, with their chubby, harried parents lugging their bagged crap, trying to keep up.

"Let's not have kids." I said.

"What?"

"Nothing."

Her leg brushed the back of my calf. It was nice. Intimate. She sat at just the right height. This was cozy. I could feel the evening chill on my face, but I felt warm.

Her leg started to wander back and forth against mine, almost like she was caressing me. I pressed against her gently. I noticed her leg was vibrating. A soothing hum. A purr. I glanced down and saw both pairs of legs stretched out in front of us.

I jumped off my seat as a dark furry form screeched and bolted out from beneath our bench. Jessie jumped too.

"Was that a cat?" She asked.

"You saw it?" I asked.

"I saw something."

"You really saw it?"

"Yeah. Really. You okay?"

"Just a minor panic attack. Nothing to see here."

"Should we go?"

"We can. Do you need to be home?"

"Before ten."

Almost on cue, the lights of the wharf started winking out. "What time is it?" She asked.

I checked my watch "Crap. Five minutes to." I'd have given anything for another hour, "I'll walk you back to your car."

We had to hurry, as she parked at the other end of the beach, past the boardwalk. I didn't want to get her in trouble, so as much as I wanted to saunter around and enjoy the evening some more, the responsible voice in my head insisted we pick up the pace so we could go out again.

"This is me." She said, stopping in front of a dingy red Jeep. "I really had a great time." She said, looking up at me.

"Me too."

" I get off at eight tomorrow."

"Oh?"

"Oh?" She mocked, then laughed.

"I'll meet you at work."

She smiled and kissed me. I pulled her close to. It felt - right.

Our lips parted, and we rested our foreheads together. I reveled in her closeness, her scent, her voice.

"I have to go." She whispered.

"I know."

We didn't move.

"Really."

"I know." I sighed.

"Sam," she said gently.

I took a deep breath, and with tremendous effort, stepped back with both of her hands in mine.

"See you tomorrow." I said.

"Oh?" she mocked again.

We both laughed.

She let go of my hands, stepped into her Jeep, and closed the door, then she started the engine. Cutting Crew's "I just died in your Arms Tonight", issued from her radio.

"Tomorrow." She said with a grin.

I smiled back. "Tomorrow."

She backed out of her space, then drove out of the gravel lot.

She had to pass me again on the street and waved.

I stood alone, with what my grandpa would've called a "shit-eating grin."

The night seemed a little darker, a lot colder.

I turned to start the walk toward home.

Somewhere in the night, a cat screamed.

"Shut up!" I commanded. Nothing was going to ruin this night.

15

SHIT GETS REAL

THE STORM RAGED AS I STOOD UPON THE SHORE. WAVES SWELLED, then crashed into each other in a chaotic, thunderous dance. The cat perched at my feet on the sand, untouched by the wind and the rain. It simply passed through as her unsettling green glow illuminated her form and nothing else. She meowed - at least I think she did, I couldn't hear anything over the storm's chaos - then she stepped out onto the water, walking just a short way before a massive wave rose and crashed down on top of her, swallowing all but her otherworldly light which held steady, glowing as she strolled through the murky liquid.

Lightning illuminated the world in a blinding flash, revealing the lighthouse looming over me, The island was impossibly close - just a few treacherous yards away. A stream gushed down the weathered staircase - a jagged scar cut into the rock's scabrous face.

I stumbled back from the edge of the sea, desperate to get away.

From atop the tower, the powerful light blazed to life, searching the waves and the sand around me. The beach offered no protection. I lost my footing and fell backward.

The beam's cold light caught me, penetrated my body, revealing my insides as if I were transparent. Lost in the light's blinding glare, the cat hissed impatiently from above.

Why had I returned to this place over and over again? It was as if, no matter how hard I resisted, the lighthouse kept drawing me back. There was no use trying to escape. I was tiny, weak, ephemeral, while the lighthouse was permanent, stalwart, implacable. Long after I was gone and forgotten, it would be here, a solid fact standing forever, a fixed point between worlds, anchoring water, land and sky - reality, fantasy, and spirit.

There was no point resisting. I could as well fight the passage of time.

So, resigned to my fate, I surrendered to the only course open to me. I got back on my feet, steadied myself and stepped forward.

—————-

I jolted awake in a dark room with the dream replaying in my head. Sleep was out of the question with it dominating my thoughts. What did it mean? What did it have to do with Christine? Was it really just a dream or something else?

I needed to talk. I needed Max. I shuffled through the house and quietly pushed open the door to my room. The dim moonlight coming through the window showed an empty bed. Max wasn't here.

The clock on my nightstand read 1:04.

Confused, I checked Gram's room. It was empty too.

Now wide awake, I returned to the living room and looked out the window. Max's truck sat parked at the curb.

I switched the light on to help me think and saw on top of the coffee table, along with my clothes, a large black wallet, out of which jutted a slip of paper. The wallet was heavy and flipped open as I lifted it, revealing a silver-and-gold police badge. Opposite was an ID card that read, *Raphael Morales, Detective.*

With shaking hands I unfolded the paper.

You took my family.
Now I got yours.
-Lester

Cold fear swept over me as I struggled to make sense out of what was right in front of me. My thoughts careened through recent events: Christine Dunn, the crazy woman in the street, my panic attacks, the dreams about the lighthouse. They all led me to one conclusion;

We hadn't beaten Lester at all. We'd just pissed him off.

I struggled with the reality of the situation. It wasn't fair. Why was this happening to me? He'd picked the fight with us, attacked us in the lighthouse when all we wanted was to get out of the storm.

It was the first time I'd ever stood up to anyone. Wasn't that supposed to be a good thing? This one time, I'd faced something I truly feared, and now, Gram, Max, her dad, and hell, maybe even Christine Dunn were paying for it. Max always said I was a pussy. Maybe pussies aren't supposed to take on scary things. Maybe the reason we don't stick up for ourselves, is that deep down, we know we'll just fuck up.

If I'd only checked the weather report that night. Read the signs. Followed my instincts.

My thoughts spiraled as I realized the harm I'd caused by my mistake. Now, I didn't have any choice. If Max and Gram had a chance, it was up to me. I had to make it right.

"Why don't you grow a pair and learn to drive?" The words echoed in my head as I sat behind the steering wheel in Max's truck.

I promised myself that if I somehow got through this, I'd do as she said.

In school, they'd taught us how to drive in a sedan equipped with an automatic transmission, and chicken brake for the instructor, and three other students heckling from the backseat. Those lessons from a few years ago, weren't going to help me drive this beast of a truck with a stick shift.

I stepped on the clutch as I'd seen Max do a bunch of times, and turned the ignition. It rumbled to life.

Encouraged, I eased it forward. The truck lurched violently and died.

I killed it two more times before I remembered to release the emergency brake. Then, a few more times after that, as I fought to coordinate the foot pedals. I had to get going. My family was counting on me. But the more I tried, the more flustered I got.

Max made it look so easy. Like she didn't even think about it.

I took a breath, and tried to channel my best friend. "Come on you fucking, pansy-ass excuse for a rusted-out, piece of shit!" I turned the key, released the clutch, and gave it some gas. It bucked once and then once again before smoothing out, and we advanced up the street.

I made a deal with myself - no stopping. If I stopped, I'd probably never get it started again. Luckily, it turned out that this late at night, it wasn't a problem.

As I got closer to my destination, an idea took shape, one Max would've loved.

A few minutes later, shaken and surprised to be in one piece, I arrived at the marina.

The gravel rumbled under the tires as I rolled into a parking space and stopped. I'd made it. Bitchin'. Good for me. I switched off the car and took a couple of deep breaths.

I looked over at my crutches leaning against the seat next to me and decided they wouldn't be much help. I climbed out and limped down to the docks and continued past the empty cleats where, for years, we'd secured my grandfather's skiff. Soon, I was deep in a forest of sailing masts jutting up from expensive floating toys, and stood before Mitch Kavanaugh's yacht.

Technically I suppose, it belonged to his dad.

Like I cared.

I climbed aboard and worked my way to the cockpit.

I prayed Kavenaugh was smug enough to assume no one would dare steal his boat. I found the key stashed in a cup holder next to the captain's chair, attached to a small, yellow flotation device that read, *Sailors Get You Wetter*.

I'd never driven a boat this big, but I'd spent plenty of time on the water. No clutches or brakes to muck with. This was my element.

Moving as quickly as I could, I untied the lines, got myself back behind the huge silver wheel and put it in reverse. My leg complained at all the movement but I couldn't think about that now.

She backed out smooth and steady. I pointed the nose in the right direction, and started forward, easily threading my way out toward the open sea.

Regulations required that boats go slow near the docs, so the wake didn't damage the vessels moored in their slips.

Again - like I cared.

With the running lights off, I hurried away from the other boats and opened it up, full throttle as soon as I was clear.

I arrived at my destination all too quickly and dropped anchor. Kavanaugh may've been a first-rate douchebag, but I couldn't bring myself to wreck his boat on the tiny rock landing. The lighthouse loomed over me, like some ancient, crumbling medieval tower, I stepped onto the swim platform on the back, and without letting myself think about it, dove into the water. The cold shocked the air out of my lungs, I broke the surface and inhaled in quick, ragged gasps.

My clothes restricted my limbs, making my progress slow and awkward but finally, my fingers brushed against slimy, jagged stone and I climbed up the gradual incline until I stood shivering on the slippery shelf.

After one brief look back to the yacht, floating safely just a little ways off, I turned and headed for the next obstacle - the stone steps that led up, away from the relative safety of the water.

The last time I'd made this climb, I'd had to battle wind, rain, and lightning. Now, all I had to contend with was my fear of heights and a half-healed hole in my leg.

I kept my head down, keeping my eyes on the steps, so I wouldn't look out at the water below and stop dead.

About two-thirds of the way up however, I gave in to the urge and allowed myself a quick glance. I froze - surprisingly not out of fear, but because I was awestruck. The stars shone brilliantly, reflecting off the water around me, so it seemed I stood inside a sea of constellations, with the milky way shimmering across it. I continued again and it seemed rather than climbing, I dove, deeper and deeper into the center of well, everything - tiny and insignificant, sure, but also a vital part of this endless, living cosmos.

Great views aside, I knew that at best, I was offering myself as a sacrifice for the lives of my loved ones. At worst, I was throwing away my life, away along with theirs - just another log tossed onto the fire. I was probably going to die. I was sure of it. Maybe that's why I enjoyed the view. Without hope, what did I have to fear?

Soon - sooner than I expected, anyway - I stepped with quivering legs onto the summit, the flat expanse upon which the lighthouse stood, and really felt as if I'd entered the heart of creation, with the lighthouse nearby, at its nexus.

Were I to describe it, I'd say it was a short fat tower squatting atop a crumbling cube - a hodgepodge of peeling white paint, peppered with off-color age spots and running rivulets of rust, sitting on a pimple a rock, covered with bird crap. There were folks who loved this building. They considered it a fading treasure from another age, a monument to ingenuity and plucky determination. I thought it was ugly. I always had.

But now it seemed a part of the endless wonder I beheld. The beauty overwhelmed me.

I staggered forward. The ground crunched under my wet shoes and brought me back to myself. I had a job to do.

The front door, also painted white, bore deep scars, as if someone had taken an axe to it, exposing the dark wood beneath.

Had we closed it when we'd left? I didn't remember.

Images of what I might find flooded my mind, but I tried to push them away as I approached.

The knob, its mechanism eaten by decades of exposure to salt air, resisted my effort to turn it. I grasped it with both hands, gritted my teeth and tried again. The metal, pitted with rust, ripped at my skin. I leaned into it, refusing to give in. Finally, I was rewarded with a ragged screech, and it turned. Steeling myself, I took a deep breath, and shouldered the door open. The hinge creaked as it swung slowly inward.

Starlight illuminated the first few feet; revealing dark puddles and shards of plaster littering the floor. Everything beyond hid in complete darkness. It was exactly how I remembered.

I stepped inside.

There was no gunshot. No shadowy figure hid in the shadows, but where the outside air was fresh and brisk, effervescent with the smell of salt and life, the inside reeked of decay and death. As my eyes adjusted, I made out familiar cracks running along the plaster walls. The ceiling marred by holes, both large and small.

This was the room where the fight had taken us - the last confrontation between Lester and his daughter, Suzy.

There was no point in trying to be sneaky. The door had announced my presence. Tentatively, I called out, "Hello?" My voice echoed back.

Jagged pebbles crunched beneath my shoes as I stepped across the room and through the next doorway. I didn't have a flashlight. I was led by instinct and memory.

I now stood in the rotunda, beneath the tower. An iron staircase spiraled up the wall toward the lamp room above. I stepped in a puddle. The water crested the tops of my shoes.

Past this point, darkness swallowed everything. Had someone stood directly in front of me, I wouldn't have known it.

I touched the wall to orient myself, then stepped into the hallway. To my left lay the kitchen where we'd spent most of our time. To my right was the bedroom where Lester had hidden his family's remains. I stopped and called out again, "Gram? Max?"

I stood completely still, listening for any movement, breathing, anything. I heard nothing except the soft surf outside.

I pushed forward cautiously, one hand on the wall, the other out in front.

My steps echoed soggily.

I came to a second bedroom on my right. I stopped, and again I called out, "Hello? Anyone?"

Again, nothing.

The final room waited just a few steps further, at the end of the hall.

Dim light peaked through a window missing its plywood board and showed—nothing. No bodies. No Lester. No - anything.

The place was fucking empty! What the hell was going on? Was this a joke? The lighthouse was the most obvious place to take them. My dreams had directed me here. How had I fucked up? Why the hell hadn't Lester left an address, if he wanted me to come find him? How long would he wait before he started killing?

"Hello? Anybody?" I tried a final time.

Finally, I was answered. A cry - sad, longing - the lonely yowl of a beast trapped alone, echoed from somewhere back down the hall. If I were to describe the sound of desperate, hopeless sadness, it would be this.

I retraced my steps.

It cried again. This time with a sense of urgency, or anger. Perhaps both. I followed it to the first bedroom and paused in the doorway.

I saw nothing at first. Just thick, inky blackness. Then, a green glow faded into view, floating near the floor several feet away - more like a smudge than a source of light. It remained in one spot. Half of it held still, while the other half, flicked back and forth.

It meowed once, then as I watched, it faded. Disappeared. I scanned the room, behind me, up, down, It was gone.

Something bit my ankle. I yelped and jumped back into the hall. It appeared in the doorway, cried again, then glided back into the room, returning to the same spot as before.

"Fine," I said, rubbing my leg. I got the hint. It seemed to have something to show me. It was Eartha Kitty, but fuzzy, out of focus. Just an amorphous glob of hazy green light. I followed it cautiously. Still keeping close to the wall, trying to remember where the decaying furniture was placed. I remembered a small chest of drawers leaning against the wall, and wasn't surprised when I brushed against it's surface. I went around it and continued down the wall. My shin collided with something solid. It turned out to be the old bed frame.

I couldn't look away from the glow. It drew my gaze, as it was the only thing in the room I could see. It hovered before the place where we'd discovered Suzy's remains and those of her family. Encased in ceramic urns and sealed in the wall.

It floated away as I approached. I knelt on the cold floor and ran my hand along the rough plaster until I found the hole. Tentatively, I reached in, mindful of the jagged edges of broken lathe behind the plaster. I passed my hand back and forth, over the gritty surface and came up empty.

I pulled my hand out and straightened. "There's nothing here."

The glow screeched and flowed toward me.

"Okay!" I stuck my hand in again, but this time moved it slower, moving it forward and back, methodically, overlapping the ground with each pass, fighting the urge to hurry. In the corner, at the back of the hole, something shifted under my hand. I fumbled for it, clutched it, and drew a tiny cube that fit in the palm of my hand. Eartha Kitty evaporated as I stood up.

I stuffed the treasure in my pocket, sure that if it dropped in the darkness, I'd never find it again and rushed outside to stand for a moment in the cool, free air.

There, I pulled the object from my pocket. It was a simple, black cardboard box. The lid lifted off easily, and inside lay a delicate gold chain. I lifted it out of the box. Dangling on the end, glimmering gold in the moonlight, was a delicate four-leaf clover.

Jewelry? What the hell? I'd just wasted hours while he did who-knows-what to the people I loved and I had no idea where they were.

I stuffed the trinket back into my pocket and rushed down the stairs as fast as my leg would let me, my mind scrambling to figure out where there were.

Santa Carla wasn't a huge town, but there were countless places they could be. Where would a psychotic spirit have taken…

It occurred to me that I'd come here because that's where the story took place for me. But for Lester, he'd started his killing spree somewhere else. When his wife left him, she'd fled up into the nearby mountains. Boulder Creek wasn't far away, just a half hour's drive, but it was rural - a small, tight-knit community tucked into the redwoods. Maybe that's as far as she could go with her limited resources. Maybe she'd planned to hide out there while she figured things out. Whatever her reasoning, he'd still tracked her down before she could take her next step.

Maybe that's where he'd gone, but how could I know for sure?

I stepped down onto the landing. Kavenaugh's boat was anchored just a few yards away - a trained dog on its leash. I waded down the slippery incline into the sea, and swam back to the boat.

The freezing water brought clarity. It would've been damned hard for Lester to've gotten everyone here. Gram would not have done well in this icy water, or the climb afterward. I was stupid for not realizing that before. What's more, I'd assumed the cat was aligned with Lester. Trying to get revenge on Max. But what if that wasn't the case? She hadn't really done any harm either time I'd seen her and hadn't interacted with Max at all. What if she had her own agenda?

I arrived at the boat and pulled myself onto the swim platform. God I was cold.

My teeth chattering, I pulled up the anchor, climbed behind the wheel and headed back to the docs.

Lester must have gone back to where this had all started. Not where it started for us, but to his starting point, the place where this chapter had really begun for him.

16

A REUNION

I docked Kavanaugh's boat, quickly secured it, and headed up
the ramp. I managed to coax Max's truck back onto the road, and
so I wouldn't kill the engine again, decided to continue ignoring the
stop signs. The result was a few honked horns, but thankfully, no
stalls or crashes, as I approached the freeway onramp.

Accepting that I was going to have to go past second gear, I
pulled Max's truck onto Highway 17 and headed east.

I've heard that for some people, driving can be relaxing. They
get in the car, their minds wander, and they don't notice the passing
miles as they listen to music.

I got the truck up to forty miles an hour, headed up into the
hills, and despite keeping to the right lane was the target of more
blasted horns and middle fingers.

I'd like to say I used the time to invent a plan - some way to get
everyone free, assuming they were still alive - without getting myself
killed. I'd like to say things were looking more hopeful as I got closer
to my destination. Sure, I'd like to say that.

Thank God I have a necklace, I thought sarcastically. Maybe I could
strangle him with it.

I hadn't really experienced hopelessness before. When my

parents died, there wasn't any time for hope or fear or anything. One minute I was trying to sleep in the back seat of our station wagon, and the next we were careening off the road, diving toward the water.

I'd lived with my grandparents ever since.

I white-knuckled my way into the hills, railing against the unfairness of it all. Asking different variations of *why me?*

That's right, I spent the entire drive feeling sorry for myself. Some hero.

When I was a kid, my grandpa used to drive us up to Boulder Creek on Sunday mornings for breakfast. We'd stop at a little place in town called The Treehouse Cafe, and I'd have french toast and listen to the river as it rushed by.

I knew I could find my way there. After that, I wasn't sure. I didn't have an address, just a six-year-old's memories of her house and the street where it stood.

I took the turn-off and wound my way into the trees, searching for something that looked familiar, knowing that over thirty years had passed since she'd died, and since then things had changed quite a bit. Finally, after trying about a dozen streets, I veered onto the correct one. I can't tell you how I knew, it just felt familiar.

I parked across the street and switched off the engine. Detective Morales' brown Nova sat in the driveway. I'd come to the right place. Even after decades, with a new hedge bordering the front yard, and a tree now standing tall in the middle of the grass, I still knew it right off, as if it'd been my house.

The zen-like feeling I'd had earlier had evaporated. Now that I was here, I was terrified, scared for my own life, sure, but what was worse, if I failed, Gram and Max would pay for it. The two people I'd always counted on for help, who I'd leaned on in the past, were here - depending on me.

I had this image in my head, which I absolutely knew was real - Gram and Max both dead on the floor, and Lester, that twisted psychopath, wearing Mr. Morales' body like a suit of armor, waiting for me to come in and see it for myself.

I didn't stand a chance. Maybe it would be better if I just drove away. He wanted to take everything away from me, to prove I was powerless. He wanted his revenge.

If I didn't walk through that door and see whatever he'd done, he'd never get the satisfaction.

At least I could claim that small victory. I could keep that small triumph from him.

Gram wouldn't want me to go in there. She'd feel better knowing I'd kept myself safe, wouldn't she?

Then, I heard my grandfather's voice in my head, and he wasn't pleased. "Face your mistakes. Be a man, and own up to your responsibility."

Then I heard Max's voice. "Quit being a pussy and get your ass in there."

I turned off the motor and got out. Feeling like I was underwater - Icy water - I shivered as I crossed the street in my damp clothes. My heart beating like rhythmic thunder in my ears.

I arrived at the door and pushed it open.

It was different from Suzie's memories, and yet familiar.

Max and Gram sat across from me in plush, peach-colored chairs, leaning forward awkwardly, with their hands behind them. Two people were on the couch next to me facing them - Bunny, Max's step-mother and to my horror, Jessie too.

In the middle of the room lay two bodies, a man and a woman, crumpled on top of each other. Their blood stained the shag carpet underneath.

"Look who's here. Hey, Kipper, You took your time. We got started without you." His words spit at me through Gram's mouth. Her wrinkled chin jutted out as he leered at me through her eyes. Cocky. Triumphant. Mocking.

Her face was a caricature. She squinted as though she'd spent years working outside in the glaring sun, and she spoke through a mocking smile, her tongue attacking the back of her teeth, over-emphasizing each consonant. I hadn't heard her voice in years, since Grandpa died. Now, Lester forced her to speak, using his words, his inflections. He'd taken everything dear to me and was corrupting it.

I'd walked in, positive I was going to die, sure that it would be for nothing, but the way he used her - it flipped a switch. The fear and doubt were swept away. In its place was the cold, hard truth. Lester was going down.

"Have you figured it out yet? How I tracked everybody down?" Her body relaxed suddenly.

Max shook her head violently then her eyes flashed open. The corners of her mouth rose in a jeering smile. "It was you."

I didn't say anything.

Lester's smile widened. He was enjoying this.

Bunny - Max's stepmother - turned so I could see her face. Black streaks ran down from her eyes, and she had a large purple bruise on her left cheek. Her hair, bleached blonde and usually teased high and wide, was unkempt. Wild. "You gave me the ride back to shore." She giggled, then hunched forward as if her spine had lost its integrity. "Please, stop this!" she pleaded.

"Shut the fuck up, Bunny. He wants us to beg." Now *that* sounded like Max. She jumped to her feet. "Sam, get the fuck outta here."

From a doorway behind her strode a short powerful form dressed in slacks and a too-tight sport coat. He beelined to Max and backhanded her across the face. She fell back into her chair. Her eyes filled with hate.

He turned toward me, his gun bouncing in its shoulder holster. A blood-stained bandage covered his cheek. It was Max's dad - well, his body, anyway. He looked exhausted. Worn out. "How does it feel? You brought me to everyone here."

"What do you mean?"

"Seriously? You can't figure it out? How do you think I got back?" He reached out a hand and with his dirty finger, drew a line down Jessie's cheek.

She wore the same light pink sweater as she had on our date. She drew back, quivering.

"My new family," he said.

"I came," I said, "just like you wanted. Let them go."

His face went slack.

"That's not going to happen." Jessie's face stretched into Lester's stringy version of a smile.

"Stop it." My voice sounded thin and impotent.

Lester's joyless laugh vomited out of her mouth. "This is going to be fun. The things I could tell you. So many secrets. Should I start with your gram? Nah, that's too juicy. How about your best friend? Or better yet, your girlfriend."

While Jessie focused on me. Detective Morales knelt next to Max's chair and whispered something. He reached for her face and gently touched the cheek he'd just punched.

"Te quiero," she whispered back.

Jessie's eyes widened. Her body crumbled. Her cruel smile dissolved into sobs.

Max's dad went rigid and stood up. "I have something for you," he said, then left the room

"I'm so sorry," I whispered.

If only I'd been stronger.

Max and I locked eyes. There was hate, yes. But also an ice-cold resolve.

He came back carrying a cardboard box. "Presents." He seemed almost giddy as he set the box on the dead man's back. He pointed at the corpses. "Don't you love what they've done with the place?" He laughed as he opened the flaps and drew out a cylindrical-shaped item wrapped in newspaper.

He pulled the paper off with a flourish, exposing a shiny black finish.

"A vase?" Jessie asked.

"An urn," Max corrected, bleeding from the corner of her swollen lip. She eyed Lester. "You got another friend in there?"

Lester smiled. "Soon enough." He pulled out another.

"He's got one for each of us." I realized.

He pulled out another and held it up. "Ding-ding. Give that little shit a prize."

"What?" Bunny said, her face horrified.

Lester giggled as he dug back into the box. "You know, I used to think I needed the whole body."

Max didn't skip a beat. "You're fucking kidding me."

"Nope. People get all dizzy-like when they die. It takes 'em a while to get their bearings." He added another to the growing pile. "I just need a little piece - something they're attached to - a finger, toe, eyeball…" He chuckled again. "Add a little willpower - I've got plenty of that - and you'll never know what's happening until it's done."

He lifted the fourth and final urn out of the box. He lurched forward. The urn dropped from his hand, landing on the others with a hollow thunk.

Gram's leg recoiled and as he pivoted toward her, she struck out again, catching him in the side of the face.

He fell forward again, landing on the corpses.

"You bit—" He pushed himself up, turning around as he reached for his gun. Jessie kicked him in the back of the head, while Max's heavy boot smashed into his face. He fell again.

Gram stood up. Max and Jessie followed, and they continued stomping down on his head and the upper body.

Only Bunny kept her seat. "Stop it! You're killing him," she screamed.

Struggling with the uneven surface, trapped under the tangle of legs and feet pounding down on him, he covered his head with one arm, with the other, he jerked out his revolver.

Without thinking, I dove toward him, over the couch.

Thunder exploded. I landed on him hard, the wind burst from my lungs.

I reached for the gun, but he wrenched it to the side, then drove his elbow into my eye.

My head rang from the impact. The left side of my face went numb. Half-blind, desperate, I grabbed his gun hand and clasped it in both of mine - trapping the weapon - and hung on.

Max stomped down hard on his face. There was a crack and he recoiled.

His grip loosened. I ripped the gun away and rolled, taking it with me. It slipped out of my bloody hands and flew over the back of the couch.

"Fuckin' A!" said Max.

Lester raised himself onto his hands and knees. Max, Gram, and Jessie redoubled their assault until, finally, overwhelmed, he collapsed on top of the corpses.

"Get his keys!" Max shouted.

Still fighting for breath, I pushed him onto his back. He rolled off the dead couple and lay on the carpet, his face was a mask of blood and bruises.

I slipped his keyring from his pants pocket.

Still half-blind, my hands quivering. I fumbled through the keys, then held up the smallest one.

"That's it," she said.

I hobbled over to Gram. "You're amazing," I said.

She smiled and turned her back to me so I could get at the 'cuffs. "So are you," she said.

I freed her, then moved on to Max and Bunny.

I paused for a moment to catch my breath. My side ached.

Gram grasped my shoulder and looked into my eyes. "Are you okay?"

I nodded. "It's good to hear your voice."

I freed Jessie. She spun and wrapped her arms around me.

I stumbled under her weight, but happily returned the hug. I couldn't believe we'd survived. "Gram, this is Jessie," I said, after we'd let go of each other.

"I'm his girlfriend,"

Gram's smile evaporated. "Sam, you're bleeding." She stepped toward me. I looked down. Blood covered the lower half of my shirt. I raised it up and saw a small hole just above my left hip, blood pumping to the rhythm of my pulse.

Jessie gasped, "You've been shot."

"This isn't over." Max had retrieved her father's gun and stood before the window. Her hands trembled as she pulled the hammer back. It clicked with deadly finality.

"Max, what are you doing?"

"It's not Max," Bunny yelled.

"I'm me, you fucking dipshit." She wiped a tear with the back of her hand, then pointed the revolver down at her father's head. "We'll do like he said. We'll cut off his finger and put it in one of those goddamned things."

"No!" Bunny screamed.

The room darkened around the edges. I struggled to focus.

"Sweetie, you don't know what you're doing. You're just going to trap your father," said Gram.

I couldn't track what everyone was saying. Their voices were so far away. I felt foggy. Disengaged. Dizzy.

Max lowered the pistol. "What do we do?" She tottered and fell backward, barely missing the window. Lester gripped her ankle. He let go and launched himself on top of her. Before she could react he punched her face twice, then tore the gun from her hands.

My legs gave out and I suddenly I was on the couch. Disconnected from everything going on around me. My damp clothes no longer carried a chill. In fact, I felt warm, comforted, as if I was wrapped in a thick blanket. I eased back into the cushions, glided into a cloud.

No longer invested in the fight playing out before me, my mind was free to float off on its own. I remembered the first time I met Max, and watched as she beat up the guys harassing me in the hallway.

I noticed everything - the posters on the hallway walls, the flickering fluorescent lights, and *S.M. gives good head* scratched in jagged letters on one of the lockers. How, when Max swung her backpack filled with metal parts at his head, Kavenaugh's eyes drifted up so that all I could see were the whites. They fluttered a moment, then they closed and he collapsed on the ground.

I relived my first meeting with Jessie, and noticed as the sun, streaming in through the windows, highlighted her chestnut hair, reflecting rainbows off individual strands as Kavenaugh assed off, and Charlie standing behind her, stepped away from the grill, and quietly grabbed a bat from behind the register. Once Max sent the idiot on his way, he set it down and went back to work.

I traveled further back to Suzie's vision - how we'd been playing, Elisabeth, Mom, and me, in the front yard. I chased my little sister with the garden hose, The water sparkled infinite colors in the sunlight, then splashed down onto the dirt and made an intricate design in splattered mud on our feet. Mom, smiling simple joy, joined in, tickling both of us and then, "Hello Ladies." Lester just appeared. Tiny capillaries covered his nose and cheeks, inflamed by overexposure to the sun. I noticed for the first time, the stained teeth in his cruel smile, and the golden glimmer of the charm at his neck - a simple clover hanging on the delicate thread of a necklace.

The scene continued to play out, as mom sent us into the house. The door slammed behind.

Hot pain shot through my body. I opened my eyes. I was back on the couch with Jessie's hand pressed against my wound. It was agonizing. I batted it away.

"Sam." She replaced her hand and the pain again stole my breath. I contorted, and again pushed her away, then dug the small box from my pocket.

Jessie reached for my wound again.

I snatched her wrist in my weak hand. "Grab an urn."

"Sam, you're bleeding."

I stared into her eyes. "An urn." My voice sounded softer than I expected.

The closest one lay in front of Bunny, who was completely absorbed in the fight.

Max and Lester struggled on the ground, fighting savagely for control of the gun.

Jessie set the urn in my lap.

I unscrewed the lid, and pulled the charm out of the box.

"Lester." my voice sounded weak, thin. He pushed the gun toward Max's forehead. His foot kicked against mine.

I stomped down hard on his ankle. "Lester," I said again.

His head whipped toward me.

"Recognize this?" I dangled the clover for just a moment over the urn, letting him get a good look, then let it fall. It struck the rim lightly, then disappeared inside with a hollow tink, the chain snaking in after.

"No!" he screamed. He lunged toward me.

With Lester's attention split, Max ripped the weapon from his grasp. He turned back and reached for it. An explosion of thunder and fire sent him careening back into my legs. I crashed back against the sofa.

Unsure what had happened, I lay still. Waiting for the next blow. It didn't come. I opened my eyes. All was quiet.

Sitting on the floor, her face covered in blood, Max held the smoking pistol, still aimed at her father.

Screams - blood-stopping, heart-rending - stabbed into my foggy head.

It was Bunny.

Her screeching intensified, taking on a raw, savage tone.

Gram stepped over the carnage and slapped her - hard, then gathered her in her arms. "I'm sorry baby. So sorry."

Stunned silence followed, then dissolved into sobs.

Still holding Bunny, Gram addressed the room. "We're not done."

No one moved.

She kissed Bunny's forehead, squeezed her hands, then turned to face us, "Come on," she held out her arms.

Not knowing what else to do, I laid the urn on top of Detective Morales' body, and on wobbly legs, stood between Max and Jessie.

Max seemed lost, not knowing what to do with the gun.

Jessie stepped forward and gently pried it from her fingers, then laid it on the couch behind us.

We took our places in a tight circle. Gram stood opposite me, between Max and Bunny. Everyone joined hands.

Gram addressed the room solemnly. "Lester told us what to do. Picture him going into the urn. Close your eyes. Focus on it."

I closed my eyes.

"Lester, the urn is calling to you." Gram said, in a dreamy voice. "Go to it."

I pictured his spirit as a shimmering green cloud of acrid smoke, flowing out of Max's dad and into the urn. I put all of my effort into the visualization.

She repeated again. "You'll be safe, Lester. Go "

In my image, the smoke wavered, flowing past the urn, then it banked, and headed toward me. I fought the urge to use my hands to fend it off. I imagined the urn as a vacuum, sucking at his vapor trail.

"Everybody concentrate," Gram whispered. "Lester - the urn - go to it. You'll be safe."

I could feel it wasn't working. He'd said he had plenty of willpower.

The vapor didn't stop, but instead it grew and enveloped me. Suddenly, I stood in a hospital room, looking down at my own body as I slept, my face was marked with scrapes and bruises. I stared out through Detective Morales' eyes. He seethed, furious that Max'd almost died. Lester was there too, subtly adding heat to the detective's anger.

"You little shit," he screamed.

I watched my eyes snap open. I looked confused. Weak.

Lester turned up the fire on the detective's anger, driving him to grab my hospital gown as he screamed into my face.

Suddenly, I was in a different body - female. I felt insecure. Worried. Suspicious. Again, I shared the space with two different beings - Lester's familiar presence lurked in the background, heightening my anxiety. We inhabited Bunny's body as she dug through a garbage can, just outside her back door. Her perfect coral manicure was marred by moist coffee grounds and bits of eggshell. The can reeked of rancid tuna casserole.

Lester drove her on as she dug deeper, past banana peels and used tissues and discarded cat litter. Finally, underneath that, she found a red, oil-stained shop rag, folded into a wad. She unwrapped it and picked up Eartha Kitty's collar. Lester's joy grew as he made the connection for her: Max had killed her cat.

She snatched up the collar, and, wearing pink slippers and a matching robe, marched back into the house toward Max's room.

Lester had somehow hitched a ride back with us. Working quietly, he'd played us like puppets, choreographing events until they'd led us here. We never stood a chance.

How can you defeat someone who can be anywhere - who can hide in your own skin and make you do whatever he wants?

He'd killed so many people, then fed on their essences like a mosquito feeds on blood, and each one had made him stronger. What were we? How could we hope to win?

"Focus." A voice said. It was gruff, but faint.

Jessie squeezed my hand and then squeezed again, harder. I opened my eyes. I was back in the room, surrounded by everyone I cared about.

I tried to squeeze her hand, but I couldn't. Lester had grabbed the tiller and I could only watch as he made me do whatever he wanted. Gram, Max, Jessie, and Bunny were all in danger from me, and had no way of knowing. I couldn't warn them. It was only a matter of time before I picked up the gun and killed everyone I loved.

"Dammit, don't give up." A voice murmured.

Lester's influence crept over me like a slow-moving, unstoppable shadow as he showed me how he planned to do it. How he was going make me pick the gun up off the couch and kill Gram first; he showed me how he was going to aim it at her face and fire. Then, he was going to do the same with Bunny and Max. Jessie, he had other plans for. I boiled in impotent rage.

His giddy laughter echoed in my head.

After he was done he'd take a knife, remove pieces from each and drop it into an urn, then guide the lost spirits toward it, like a friendly angel, come to show them the way to hell.

"Listen to me." There it was again.

Why didn't he just get on with it? Why did he hesitate? Was he waiting until I couldn't bear it any longer?

He loved toying with me - with all his victims - like a cat torturing a wounded mouse before the kill.

"Goddamn it. Get off your ass." Harsh a gruff, the voice ripped into my thoughts. "Save my daughter." It was Max's dad.

What could I do? I couldn't move. Lester had complete control.

Another flash. I stood outside this very house, but it was an earlier time, decades ago. I looked down through Lester's eyes at his two daughters - the girls his wife had stolen. In his mind, she'd betrayed him. Abandoned him.

I knew this scene, because I'd seen it from the point of view of his daughter, Suzy, but why was he showing it to me? Was he trying to show how he was hurt? To show his side of the story? Did he really give a damn what I thought?

"He's distracting you. You're running out of time."

What time? I was beaten. He could make me do whatever he wanted, I thought.

"Then why hasn't he?"

When he'd taken someone over before, they'd immediately jumped at his command. What if he was still weak? What if he hadn't recovered completely from Detective Morales' death? Maybe the others were affecting him with their combined concentration.

No. This was just my mind reaching for a vague hope, the barest thread of a chance. I tried to discount it. It wouldn't go away.

I could still think, couldn't I? Maybe that was his weakness. He could try to distract me with his memories and his horror show of a plan, but ultimately, I still controlled my thoughts.

My body - the solid, physical form, would never be able to beat him. If we were going to win, it had to be with our thoughts - the strength of our minds - the power of will. He'd already said that.

This realization happened in an instant, as I felt the shadow creeping over my body. The longer I hesitated, the stronger he became, the more control he gained.

I created an image of the charm - methodically, carefully. Leaf by leaf, the simple golden clover took shape, and then I embellished it. I pictured a vein running down the center of each leaf toward the middle, where they all joined, and then led down to the tiny stem. I placed it at the bottom of the urn, shining in the dark with the whisper-thin chain snaking around it.

Next, I made it glow, illuminating the walls that curved around and sloped inward as they climbed toward the top. I fanned it into a light, and made it shine. Small imperfections in the gold became clear. Tiny scratches - the result of decades of wear - marred the surface.

Like a magnet, it drew more light to it. It grew stronger, more brilliant.

I stood over Chrissy Dunn. She recoiled underneath his pounding fists, crying out as he kicked her. I felt the sudden pain as she dug into his face with her keys. It was another of his distractions.

My fingers twitched against Jessie's hand. I hadn't done it. He was gaining control.

She squeezed my hand in response. Shit.

My head swam. I was still losing blood, but I couldn't give in. I focused on the image I'd built, denying everything else accept the charm's overwhelming light. It's power warmed my face.

Slowly, it raised itself from the floor of the urn, floating on it's own, spinning lazily, its light flashing as it revolved. I concentrated harder, fed it more power. Faster it spun and then faster still. Its brilliant light, pulsing - getting stronger, brighter, hotter.

Jessie squeezed my hand again. My clasp tightened. She thought it was me.

The glow faded. My legs trembled, they were going to give out. I pushed my feelings aside. Ignored everything else.

The clover pulsed with each revolution. Brighter, faster, more powerful. It grew larger and more brilliant, gaining strength as it grew, expanding past the walls of the urn, and still it expanded. Now, it drew power from me, feeding hungrily on whatever I had left. The light seeped into the room, reaching through my closed eyelids, and still it needed more.

Like a flashlight held against the skin, it's light penetrated me, illuminating my insides, warming my organs. I bathed in its brilliance and I let it burn its way through me.

The shadow flinched at its touch and drew back into itself. It was Lester.

When I was younger, Gram used to say, "Bad things live in the dark." She was right.

Encouraged by my success, I held nothing back, pouring everything into the charm, letting its radiance envelope me completely, inside and out.

He tried to flee. To hide. There was no place to go.

I drew strength from my success and poured even more of myself. The heat seemed to scorch my skin. He turned in upon himself like a scrap of paper, folded again, and again, and again. He became a thought. A memory. An impulse.

Surrounded by blinding brilliance, he could do nothing but cower - a mere black spot in the heart of the sun.

He was dead. I couldn't kill him. So, I came up with an alternative. I created an area around him, less intense, not quite as brilliant. As I'd increased the light before, now I built a shaft of lesser light - a shadow of a path - from my heart to the charm.

He'd shrunk into a small, dense bit of intense wrong amid the radiance of the charm.

I pushed slightly, pricking him with a sharp beam of light.

That was all he needed. He fled down the dimmer path into the heart of the urn - into the clover.

It enveloped him completely. Burning and fusing to him, until he became a part of it. The tiny bit of gold became his new host.

My eyes snapped open. The light disappeared. As if flipping a switch, it went out.

Everyone stared at me, their faces unreadable, their mouths agape.

In my arms, I cradled something. I looked down as my hands twisted the lid tight onto the urn.

We stood in silence. No one seemed to know what to do. My legs gave in. I collapsed to the floor.

"Sam." Jessie dropped down to help me.

A lone siren screamed in the distance as the rising sun warmed the sky.

17

SMOOTH SAILING

I DREAMED, NOT OF THE LIGHTHOUSE FOR A CHANGE, BUT RATHER A long stretch of sunlit grass - an unending meadow where birds danced on the breeze.

Someone approached. His tight sport jacket, cigar, and slicked hair at odds with the surroundings. It was Max's father. Here, in a dream - my dream - I could accept his presence without panicking.

"Detective Morales, how are you?" I said.

He smiled. "Not bad for a dead man."

"So, you're okay?"

"I'd rather be alive, but all things considered, yeah, I'm good. I wanted to say, you did a hell of a thing. I didn't know you had it in you."

"Uh, thank you?"

He smiled easily. Something I don't think I'd ever seen him do in life.

"Is there anything you'd like me to say to Max?"

"You're probably not going to remember this, but if you do, tell her I'm proud of her. She's a hell of a shot."

"I might leave that last part out."

"I trust your judgement."

"Anything else?"

"There's something you should know. It's about your grandmother, she…"

"Sam? Sam, wake up." The morning sunlight streamed through vertical blinds onto the pale mint walls of my hospital room. I lay in bed, but I felt like I floated above it.

Gram sat near my feet, knitting a scarf, or blanket, or one-armed sweater. I couldn't tell. "You have a visitor," she said.

Jessie stood next to me. She clasped my hand in both of hers. She looked at me the way I'd always wanted someone to look at me. I had a girlfriend! "Hey you." She leaned down and kissed me. "How do you feel?"

"Bitchin'."

"The doctor says you're going to be fine, dear." It was surreal hearing Gram talk, but that was pretty bitchin' too. Then she said to Jessie, "He's on some pretty strong painkillers." Those were pretty bitchin' too.

Someone was missing. "Where's Max?" I struggled to sit up, then realized it was too much effort.

"She's getting situated back at home, dear. She'll be by later." Gram kept her eyes down on her work.

Even in my altered state I couldn't imagine her living with Bunny. "How is she?"

Gram smiled and rolled her eyes.

"It's a shame her dad's taking the blame for everything." Jessie said.

Gram paused in her knitting. "I never liked the man, but he didn't deserve that."

"I've been meaning to ask, Mrs. Freman, the way you took control, how did you know to do that?" Jessie asked.

Gram didn't look up from her work. "Call me Gram, dear. Everybody does."

"Okay, Gram." Jessie smiled.

The door opened, and Max peaked in. "Sam's got a girlfriend." she sang.

"You can bite me." I sang back.

Gram shot me a look.

I shot one back at her.

Max backed through the door, pulling a wheelchair. "Ready for a road trip?"

"Road trip?" Jessie asked.

"He needs his rest," Gram added.

"Fuck that. Help me get him up. I've got something to show him."

In the end, it took all three of them to get me mobile. She pushed the wheelchair while Jessie wheeled my IV stand. Gram walked behind, looking amused and disapproving at the same time.

They managed to get me down the elevator and outside without being caught.

Outside, much of the parking lot was built on an incline, and they rolled me about halfway down, before Max pulled to a stop, facing a large hedge. "Okay, numb nuts, ready?"

I shrugged, still pretty much okay with everything.

She pushed me past the hedge and stopped.

"Oh, my!" Gram put her hand on her chest.

"Wow!" Jessie Said.

Words escaped me.

In front of us, parked sideways, taking up several parking spaces, was Max's truck. Behind it, perched on a trailer, shining bright and silver under the clear blue, Santa Carla sky, was my boat.

"The hull just needed a little pounding and welding and sanding and shit. Oh, and I don't think that engine's gonna give you any more trouble." She lowered her voice. "That dickwad wanted to charge rent, and a cleaning fee. I told him where he could stick it."

"Dickwad?" Gram asked.

"Dale," I said.

She nodded. "He *is* a dickwad."

Suddenly, it was hard to talk. "Max..." I held my arms out to her.

She hesitated.

"I promise I won't get a chubby or anything."

She laughed, and leaned down to hug me. "Way to make it awkward."

EPILOGUE

Flames danced within a stone ring, casting writhing shadows on the massive trunks of surrounding redwood trees. Around the fire stood six figures, cloaked in hooded robes of black. Colored gems hung from their necks, each one unique to its bearer.

A seventh figure approached. Her ruby shined its crimson light on an object cradled in her arms like an infant, swaddled in black fabric.

A worshiper whose gem reflected purple fire, stepped forward, and in a voice, both melodious and formal, welcomed the newcomer. "Mother Moon Goddess, merry meet, in peace and love."

The newcomer bowed and replied in an imperious tone, "Amethyst Dragonheart, Blessed be in life and death. I bear an item that requires the greatest care and most serious discretion." She lifted a layer of the dark cloth, displaying a portion of the object she bore.

The first woman peeked, then drew back, her hand on her chest. "This is unholy. I dare not."

"The powers of night and shadow command we keep this artifact safe and hidden."

"I pray thee, find another, more worthy than-"

Moon Goddess threw back her hood. "For crap's sake, drop the horseshit Sylvia, you're the only one who can keep this damned thing safe."

Sylvia pulled back her own cowl. "Go to Hell, Amanda. I've got a business to run…"

"You get a lot of cops coming in, looking for tarot cards or crystal balls?"

"No, and I don't want them to start now. It's hard enough, running an occult shop with the damned city council constantly blowing smoke up my ass."

"Then keep it in your home."

"My house? Are you nuts?

Amanda spread her arms. "Sylvia, we all have kids."

"That's not my problem."

"How much business would you get if you're banished?"

"You're threatening me?"

Amanda shrugged.

Sylvia straightened, and said coldly, "Alright, fine."

Amanda relaxed a little. This was the only way it could've gone.

Sylvia continued, smiling an enigmatic smile. "We'll discuss terms later."

"What terms?"

"Oh, I promise you won't like them," She pulled the cowl back over her head and accepted the urn. "Mother Moonstone." She returned to her place in the circle.

Amanda, her look unsure, and her posture, a little less regal, did likewise.

ABOUT THE AUTHOR

D.L. Strand has been - among other things - an entrepreneur, a coffee roaster, and a filmmaker.

He's worked on various film and TV productions all around the United States (Including the movie, *Us* with Jordan Peele and the TV comedy, *Abbott Elementary* with Quinta Brunson) but is happiest when he's at home, sitting in his jammy pants, in front of his computer, dreaming up truly awful things.

Storyteller's Pub
For more books and updates - join the Storyteller's Pub Newsletter:
storytellerspub.com

Like Audiobooks?
Find free audio versions of D.L.'s stories (read by the author) on Youtube:
https://www.youtube.com/@storytellerspub

youtube.com/@storytellerspub

facebook.com/storytellerspub

ALSO BY D.L. STRAND

Into the Storm

Catch - A Storyteller's Pub Featured Short

Fetch - A Storyteller's Pub Featured Short

Additional titles may be found at:

https://books2read.com/ap/8Gk196/DL-Strand

Watch for **Into the Depths**, the next book in the Tales of the Lighthouse saga. Coming soon!

www.ingramcontent.com/pod-product-compliance
Lightning Source LLC
Chambersburg PA
CBHW030551130626
46552CB00006B/2507